CANDY SHOP

A Novel

Black Cherry Publishing

Nicety

CANDY SHOP

NICETY

BLACK CHERRY PUBLISHING

Black Cherry Publishing
Copyright © 2012 NICETY
All rights reserved.
ISBN: 0615652670
ISBN-13: 978-0615652672

ACKNOWLEDGMENTS

Thank you to my family, I will love you all until the end of time. You are the air that I breathe. To my friends, thanks for keeping me afloat when I thought I would sink. To my cover model, Redd Lauren, thanks for doing your thing on the photos. You rock everyday! To my fans and many followers, I love you all more and more each day. Thank you for the love and support you deliver each day!

To book Bianca Daniels (Redd Lauren) for cover modeling contact biancaldaniels@gmail.com or www.thicktoppmodels.webs.com

DEDICATION

I would like to dedicate this book to my family and my friends who supported me and my dream of becoming a published writer. They believed in me when I didn't believe in myself years ago. I'm making you proud now! Also to my readers for without you there would be no me. I love you all!

To some very special readers who have been rocking with me and supporting me from day one, I love you all. Thanks to Latosha Scruggs, Jackie Figueroa, Lesa Jones, Yung-Lit, Tiffany Haynes, Camille Lamb, Nefertaria Ayo, Fallon Willis Blaqk and Tanisha-Phat-Phat.

To my besties. You all know who you are as I will only use first names but your love and support knows no bounds. Mario, Guillermo, Ashley H., Ashley P., and Ashley P. (Yes I meant to do that), Jeanne, Yvette, Bob, Manny "You're so silly", Arndell, Leslie, Princess, Walt, Aisha, Will, Karen, Theresa, Candice, Tiffany, Irene, Meron, Dia, Ed, Alisa, Angel, and Jermika. I want to thank you from the bottom of my heart for always supporting me and making sure that I stayed focused on the task at hand. To my husband, your love is as endless as it is timeless and for that you are my rock.

If I have forgotten anyone, know that I love you still.

More Titles from Nicety
Available on Kindle & Nook

"Never live your life in fear. Fear is the devil's gateway into your life."-Nicety

PROLOGUE

I mounted him like I was straddling a breadwinning horse. My young frail legs wrapped around his obese waist and slowly sat on his puny dick. It was short and stumpy just like him but I didn't care. I was not there to enjoy his dick. I was only there to fuck him just the way he liked. Luckily for me he liked twelve-year-old girls cause it was easy as pie sliding past his henchmen. He grabbed my young supple tits opening his mouth slightly like he wanted to suck them but was too fat to sit up to put them in his mouth.

I covered my mouth and giggled slightly at his epic failure, bouncing up and down on his ass like an all star pro. I moaned inadvertently to his bellows. His penetration was pounding into me raw, punching itself through my once virgin opening. I had a love hate relationship with his piece as I smiled leaning my head back in pain and foolish pleasure.

"Do you like this pussy, Mr.?" I asked provocatively.

"Shut up, you nasty little bitch. Now com' here and let me bite that monkey." He replied.

I reluctantly crawled off of his dick dripping juices all the way to his mouth as I sat on it rubbing my nipples to cum. It felt greater than anything I had ever experienced before. My determination not to enjoy this feeling didn't prepare me for the overwhelming sensation it sent through my body.

"Lick this pussy, you fat bastard. Do you hear me?"

"Mmhmm."

"Good. Now listen to this, you pedophile ass slob." I moaned wildly as I rode his face harder and faster. My little pussy tingled so much that it only fueled me to ride harder suffocating his nose with my ass cheeks. He began tapping out unable to breath but I could care less. "You and your flunkies entered my home three years ago unwanted. I watched from the closet as you murdered my mother who was a plain and simple nurse and my father, a loan shark with a few money problems."

He tapped my back vigorously punching to cave it in anxiously but I felt no pain. "But all of that I could forgive if it wasn't for the fact that my mother was three and a half months pregnant, you son of a bitch!"

I wrapped my legs around his head then jumped off his mouth and snapped his neck turning rapidly ensuring that I heard a nice crunch. When I untangled myself from around him I looked down at his bulging face, eyes still open. I sat there in relief that I had finally sought my revenge and avenged my family's horrid untimely death. The old geezer reeked of alcohol and primos but I sat there basking in his death never wanting to leave. Just as I began to feel right at home, his henchmen began knocking on the door rapidly. They banged so hard I could feel my heart jump with every loud thump. I quickly grabbed my clothes not even attempting to throw them on and darted out the window, stepping on branches and dirt as I crept out and into woods naked as the day I was born without a trace. I was lucky that the asshole's house was in the middle of nowhere cause it gave me time to regroup before running into any civilians.

Every time I think of that day my pride grows a little inside especially since that was the first time I had ever been broken open. Do I feel guilty? Hell no. Why should I? Death is just another part of life. If you want a nice story where the guy gets the girl and lives happily ever after in the suburbs with 3.5 children, a cat and dog, and two midsize sedans then you're in the wrong place. But if you want to hear my story, I mean really hear it, then listen. Don't just wait for your turn to speak.

5 YEARS LATER

The garbage tasted like fresh dirt and dog shit on a warm summer's day after the night's rain. Red pulled her midnight colored shoulder length hair back into a tight pony and continued digging through the garbage searching for food. Her 5' 5" stature, made it difficult for her to reach down deep to find anything good. She had been on the streets for a long time now and knew all of the good restaurants that threw out not so bad trash. Pay dirt! She was happy to have scored a half eaten slice of pizza that was surprisingly still warm. She scarfed it down not leaving a morsel behind. She licked her fingers savoring every moment of it even the pieces that were bitten off of. People walked past pointing and staring as she sat there with a chunky mouth trying to swallow the food. It wasn't the first time she was treated like sideshow attraction and frankly she didn't give a shit.

Her body was thin, having no hips but her booty was nice and round poking out as if to say hello when you saw it. Her tits were size d's but you didn't know it by looking at them as she often stole the wrong sized bras from the local thrift stores. Usually she snagged ones that were way to big, never having a chance to look at the tags. The mean streets of Chicago weren't shit to play with especially if you're a young female. It ate you up and swallowed you whole but Red, refusing to go live in a rat infested, gruel serving foster home any longer when she was twelve, learned how to survive better than most. It wasn't very often but she would even jerk men off for fifty dollars a pop. It was quick and easy money no matter how disgusting she found it. When a lame got fresh and thought he could take more, so did she, by stabbing him in the leg and twisting the box cutter. They didn't know who they were dealing with.

She walked off from the trash wrapping her arms around her body to hide her frail stature. As a short body she seemed to slip through the crowds unscathed and unnoticed. She had sought shelter many nights at a really nice mission called Olive Branch, which included Internet and telephones for free use. They were small but they had room for women and children who lived on the street and they knew Red and her story very well. Sometimes they even served great big grand feasts for the homeless when they were donated enough food. Unfortunately, today wasn't one of those days as her stomach rumbled on. She made it back to the shelter stairs and could hear yelling eroding from the corridor.

"That bitch stole my last $20!! I know she did. Now I'm not gonna put up with this shit no more. She steals from everybody and she's got to go!" The social worker Sherry was more irate than she had ever been before.

Red had never seen her so angry about losing anything. Yeah she stole the money but people usually just blew it off. They knew she was a kid and had no family so people really just felt sorry for her. It was weird to her why somebody was tripping now. She walked in the door prepared to apologize and vow never to do it again as usual. But she wasn't going to readily admit to it just yet, only when she could conjure up enough water works to do so.

"What's all the yelling about?" Red said coyly.

"You know damn well what its about. You stole my last $20 you little bitch and I needed that money for my lunches until Friday. You think you the only one struggling, huh?" Sherry said pointing closely to her face.

Red could smell the alcohol on her breath, as did everyone else knowing that she was lying. The most anyone had ever seen her eat at her desk was whipped cream and Saltine crackers. She was only mad because she had stolen her six-pack money and in Red's eyes she considered it doing her a favor. Sherry's health had deteriorated tremendously over the years but it seemed she didn't care. Her drinking had become so excessive that her skin had started to become old and withered like she was seventy years old when she was only forty. She had been in and out the hospital numerous amounts of time and had just recently got out due to her eye falling out of its socket. No doctor had an explanation as to why and was mortified by the sight but were able to push it back in and perform surgery.

"I didn't take your money. Now get that fucking finger out of my face before I bite it off, bitch." Red scowled at her with the most devilish look in her eyes.

She thought for a second about how nice and salty her finger would taste in her mouth as she drooled eagerly awaiting temptation. Sherry looked into her eyes and knew she wasn't playing then jerked her hand back quickly. She stepped back behind the building administrator holding her hand in fear. She wouldn't dare fuck with a hungry homeless person as she witnessed one man sitting in the back corner of an alley eating another man's face before. It was the most gruesome scene she had ever seen but nothing compared to the awful look in his eyes when he turned and caught her looking at him. It was like something out of a M. Night Shyamalan movie and Red had the same look.

"Get her out of here!" Sherry screamed in pure horror.

"Red, I'm sorry but this is the last time. We've given you too many chances and now this is it. It's time for you to leave." The administrator said almost afraid to speak himself.

The rest of the homeless pack had made their way outside building a crowd around the commotion. They had all been long waiting for the day Red got put out as well seeing as though she had stolen countless items from them too. I don't give a fuck! She thought as she hawked them down and rolled her eyes all ghetto like.

"Ya'll can kiss my ass. I told you I didn't fucking take that bitch's money. Sleep with one eye open!" Red threatened, pointing to Sherry as she walked off pissed that now she had no place to go at night.

All of the shelters in town were packed full by now since they have that first come first serve rule and Olive Branch was the best one anyway. The sun was setting fast and a dark street was no world for a young girl like her. She had been there and done that before nearly having to shank a fool dead in his neck just to save her twat.

She looked around for one of her prostitute friends that would pass a few Johns her way when she asked. This time she wanted to see if she could bunk with one of them on her pimp's couch for the night. He was usually cool with it being one of the rare nice ones on the track. But everyone seemed to be taking the night off being missing in action. The more she walked, it seemed, the more deserted the streets looked. It was the dead ass of summer on a Friday night and the streets eerily resembled a ghost town.

Red could feel blisters forming on her feet from being on them all day looking for food. The smell of corner restaurant foods filled the air as well as the lights leading to them. She wanted so desperately to be able to walk in there and order something so tasty so mouthwatering it would make her head spin around twice. Some dudes that were arguing in front of the gas station as she walked up Western to 67th Street abruptly interrupted her thoughts of hunger.

One of the guys, though sexy, looked oddly familiar to her but what he was holding in his hand looked even better. Red thought if she could snatch it out of his hand and break down the alley she would be set. Then she could sell it to some worthless bootleg store and be able to finally buy some grub. Her feet pounded the pavement like Godzilla, throbbing yet swiftly as she charged straight for the dude's arm. The contents were in her grasp since the two men were still engaged in their conversation none the wiser to what was about to happen. Red ran up and snatched the contents out of the guy's hand then broke out like Gail Devers running for the Olympic Gold. No matter how swift, she was caught in mid-stride not getting very far at all as the 5'9" muscular man grabbed her arm forcefully whipping her around to the angry expression on his face.

"What the hell are you doing? You fucking crazy?" He said shaking her senselessly by one arm as he gazed down into her eyes realizing who she was. "Red? Red is that you?"

Messiah recognized that pouty face from anywhere. No matter how skinny she got her chipmunk cheeks would never change. He lowered his boiling point bringing it down to a mere fizzle. Then he smiled a very charismatic smile that shone so brightly; people could've mistaken it for sunrise.

"Yeah, yeah it's me. My bad, Messiah. I didn't know it was you. I was just thinking about snatching that shit out your hand." Red rubbed her forehead as Messiah released his grip on her arm.

"Girl, what the hell you stealing cell phones for? Awe, don't tell me you buzzin' now? You on that shit, girl?" He asked stuffing the phone down in his jeans pocket.

"No, no. I just needed to sell it to get some money." She said lowering her head in shame.

Messiah came from a good family with good morals and values. His mom died giving birth to him but his dad, a successful real estate agent, sold her parents the house she used to live in. Their parents became so close that Messiah agreed to babysit Red as a part time job when he was just fifteen years old and she was eight. His dad did everything in his power to ensure Messiah and his big brother, Nicholas whom they called Danger for his love of risk-taking, stayed out of the street life and grew into responsible adults. It was a quality that made Red trust him more than anybody she ever knew especially when his dad invited her to stay with them. Her parents were obviously living some secret double lives so other relatives were unknown. But the darkness that filled Red's heart wouldn't allow her to remain under Messiah's roof with his perfect life and that's why she ran away.

Messiah was deeply hurt when she left and now seeing her again after all this time did nothing but bring back old feelings and memories. Despite her scrawny nature she was still a very beautiful girl with cheekbones as high as the sky. Her skin was riddled in acne and the smell of garbage and week old funk plagued her body but his infatuation looked past all of that. She liked the way his strong grip felt on her body before he released her. He wasn't bulky but his muscles were nicely defined and sexy enough to send chills down her spine when she saw them. His Mexican features along with his well-tapered goatee made him so sexy that she was almost ashamed to be in his presence looking like shit.

Even though her smell could've killed any animal that came near her it was mildly drowned out by his manly essence of Gucci Sport.

"Damn baby. It's like that? I hate to see you out here like that, Red." He said using his index finger to lift her head back up, looking into her gleaming eyes. They sparkled in the streetlights making Messiah want to dig deeper into her heart to find out whom she really was.

"Well, I've been taking care of myself for a long motherfucking time now, so don't worry about me. I'll be fine." Red turned cold on him really fast.

She was never able to get too close to anyone in anyway and she wasn't about to start now. He didn't know shit about the person she was now. He wouldn't understand how she had to bash chick's heads into the ground just to steal foods they wouldn't share with her or how she had to sit there while a John breathed heavily in her ear as she jerked him off. Messiah had a great life and she had no time for Mr. Perfect. She turned to walk off but was halted by Messiah's hand pulling on her arm once more.

Red quickly snatched away. "Let me go!"

"Redina Hawkins. I'm not trying to hold you up. I just think I can help you in your state of need. That's all. If what I say, don't interest you then you can get on and I'll never holla at you again. But if you're interested, I can put you on and you'll never have to live like this again." Messiah's voice was calm like the warm summer night's wind with his slight Latino accent letting the words roll off his tongue like butter.

When he spoke he looked off in the distance never giving her eye contact once but she didn't need it. He was calm yet firm, which was his way of meaning business. He shoved his hands in his pockets turning his attention on Red's tattered blue jeans and dingy white wife beater tank top wanting to shake his head at the downfall she's been on. Red was unimpressed with his so-called "savior's speech" but having no other options she looked into his face trying to feel him out and see if he was real.

"Look, I'm no hoe. I don't fuck for money. So if that's what you got in mind you can beat it."

Messiah laughed faintly. "Naw ma, I run this joint out in Burbank and…if you want a spot I'll give it to you."

"Well what would I have to do?" Red said sounding intrigued.

"Why don't you just show up tomorrow around noon and we can go from there?" Messiah said evading the question acting nonchalant about the whole thing, like it was nothing to him.

He shook up with his boys that walked up to him trying to rap a second but he put them on hold waving them away. Red was enthralled by the level of respect these dudes had for him as he slowly reached into his right pocket. He pulled out a wad of folded cash tied down with a rubber band. He unraveled the band letting the money pop up like a jack in the box but secured it tightly. Red was mesmerized by the amount of money in his hand, never having seen that much in one place in her life. She was amazed at the fact that he was comfortable with whipping it out in front of her like that knowing that she had a propensity to snatch things.

Messiah wasn't the least bit worried about anybody taking anything from him though. He always kept his best friend right behind him tucked nicely away in the back of his jeans. It was like Allstate, he never left home without it. He counted out $500 and stuffed it down Red's tank top sliding it between her voluptuous cleavage. She looked down at it not wanting to touch it just in case it was some kind of trick.

"Take that and get you some clothes and shit, you know. Get you a room and clean yourself up. I can't have you up there looking like you fresh out the garbage, you feel me." Messiah said revealing a toothpick from his mouth that he was secretly chewing on. "If you show up tomorrow, you'll be all good."

Red couldn't stop staring at the money spilling out of her cleavage. She stuffed it down deep into her bra then nodded back at him.

"What's the address?" She said walking around to the side of him out of the way of his well-dressed clean cut and mostly attractive friends.

"Be at the Candy Shop Storage on 70th and Cicero tomorrow, girl. The guy at the desk will take care of you."

Messiah walked off with his boys not even turning back to see if she was still standing there. They hopped into his shiny black Beamer sitting on Incubus rims parked over by the gas station payphone. Red's pussy throbbed harder with each step he took but suddenly grew skeptical about her role in his business. She didn't want to sell her ass anymore, Lord knows she has been there more times than she would like to imagine. But all of the money he pulled out in front her made her question what she would really do for it. She walked across the street and bought her some fried catfish with lemon pepper from the Sharks on the corner then hopped the Western bus to 95th Street. Then she took that bus to Racine Avenue, arriving at a hole in the wall, piss infested, rundown motel, The Beverly Inn.

Red wasn't about to squander away her money just in case the job didn't work out. She figured at least she'd have some loot in her pocket for a few days if nothing else. She snatched the keys to her room from the oversized cashier who was smoking a cigarette she so desperately wanted to beg for but didn't. In the shabby room, she immediately threw her things down and stripped to jumped in the shower. Washing her filthy hair and body felt so good as the soap and hot water soothed her body and the steam relaxed her muscles. The cool breeze of the room hit her body quickly, once she stepped out the bathroom. It had actually been months since the last time she was able to wash her ass in peace without someone watching or in filth.

Red went to put the chain and dead locks on the door then sat at the round corner table opening her fish and scarfing it down as if it were her last meal licking her fingers in enjoyment. It was seasoned perfectly and the guy had even given her extra mild sauce on the side for free, just as she liked it. The room had less than perfect furniture with questionable sheets on the bed and walls that looked like they had seen a great deal in their lifetime but it was warm and not the hard cold concrete she was about to rest on. Her wet hair rested easily on her back as she laid down on the bed still wrapped in the towel ready for a good night's sleep. She turned the TV on to the news, not paying it's negativity any mind as her eyes closed like she was high off of the best drug in the world, comfort.

DECEIVING LOOKS

The banging on the door rattled her brain as she jumped up startled reaching for an object to use as a weapon. Once she got it together and realized no one was in the room she yelled. "Who is it?"

"Check out time is 12pm. You ten minutes past that girly." The janitor yelled as he wheeled his mop bucket to the next room.

Red jumped up throwing on her dirty smelly ass clothes and holey shoes then shot out the door. She gritted her teeth on spending money and hailed one of the millions of empty cabs driving past on a Saturday morning. Her first stop was to the Rave clothing store in the mall. Candy Shop Storage was a quick shot for the cab to make it up the street in a breeze since the two places were literally blocks away from each other. She planned her time accordingly even though she didn't feel like she was going on a real job interview she treated it as such. Red paid the cab driver to wait outside the mall for her while she ran in for a nice all white cotton halter maxi dress and some seashell colored flats. She brought a well-supported black strapless bra to hold her girls up well secured and a super thin thong to match. She topped it off with some silver bangle bracelets and huge silver hoop earrings. She tossed her curly hair in the mirror of the store amazed at how breathtaking she looked all cleaned up.

Once she was satisfied with her look she paid grabbing some cheap sticky lip-gloss in the process and left the store. On the road, she couldn't help but think of how nice it would be to finally earn some money and make a living for herself. She had grown weary of being a ward of the streets but getting a job without an address or telephone number was basically impossible. The seats of the cab were surprisingly soft as she scooted down into it closing her eyes to relax. Her relaxation was short lived, however, when the rain and storm started pouring down just minutes away from her drop off point.

The cab pulled up in the small driveway of the Candy Shop Storage as the driver reached his middle aged hairy arm over the seat to collect the $25.72 for the ride. The price pissed Red off but she paid it nonetheless hoping that this job was a piece of cake and she could earn money fast. The rain poured hard now beating the concrete like hooves in the Kentucky Derby. She stepped out of the cab as quickly as possible attempting to keep from looking like she was just in a wet t-shirt contest, and ran inside of the cramped building office of the company. The thunder rolled heavily as if it were an end of the world natural disaster as she looked around the office and behind the counter wondering where everybody was.

It was empty but clean inside with moving boxes hung on shelves on the wall and dollies parked in the corner. The small television above the counter displayed nothing but the lot full of huge storage units and paperwork lied all along the table behind the counter. The computer underneath the TV on the counter was pitch black as if no one had been on it for a while. Her heart sank to the bottom of her stomach wondering if she had been played yet again. She was certain that this would be her big break and her life would surely change for the better. But it seemed her life was back at square one in a split second aside from the fact that she had a pocket full of cash.

The sky became almost as dark as night as lightning lit up the sky like a Christmas tree. She looked over at the door in the corner behind the counter, walking over to it slowly putting her ear to the door. There was tussling going on behind the thick door but she really couldn't hear much. Her nerves kicked in as sweat formed under her armpits and she knocked on the door rather hard making sure whomever was in there could hear her with ease. The door handle jiggled a little and out came a man with his pants hanging half way down his waist. His long braids were thick and hung past his clavicle but that didn't take away from the angry look on his hairless baby face.

"Can I help you?" The man tried to seem pleasant as to act professional but he was obviously annoyed at the fact that Red had interrupted his little rendezvous. He straightened his pants behind the counter so she couldn't peek then typed something on the computer.

"Yes, um, I'm here for my job interview." She said trying to remain in character.

"Well the boss is gone for the day, sweetie. You just missed him. You'll have to come back another day." He dismissed her as if she were a piece of trash under his shoe.

He never even looked up at her continuing to type on the computer on what looked like some weird social networking site from where she was standing. Bentley was an old kat around his late forties or early fifties, no one ever knew because he would never tell his age. You could tell he was old school by the way he spoke and by his swag. He never liked to tell his age because he looked much younger than what he was and that's how he pulled his dates. He started working for Messiah after his father died. Messiah's father needed a caregiver for the pancreatic cancer that ate away at him five years ago and Bentley was there for him every step of the way. They became so close that Messiah looked at him as another bother and kept him around as long as he stayed off that narcotic that had grabbed a hold of him. He agreed with Messiah's help and has been sassy and animated ever since.

"Um Bently, is that what your name tag says? I don't mean to be a bitch, but I was told to come here at noon so I need to speak to the manager or something because I'm not leaving here until I get this fucking job. So can you pull your dick out of your ass for one minute so I can get paid? Thanks." Red snapped placing her hand over the keyboard halting his fingers abruptly.

"There is no manager just the owner and he only hires through word of mouth and everybody he sends this way I most definitely know about." Bently rolled his eyes at her in disgust giving her the short look and pushing her hand away from his. "And he sure didn't tell me nothing about you."

He smelled his hand acting funny then turned his attention back on the keyboard. The corner door pushed open and out came another male skimpily dressed in blue booty shorts with a thin pink string thong sticking out around his waist and a red t-shirt tied up tightly to the back revealing a hairy navel.

"Boo, why you ain't come back?" The man said lacing up his Chuck Taylors then going behind the counter to rub on his companion.

"This chick came up looking for a job and I don't know why she still standing there 'cause she is too through." Bently said throwing his hand up dismissing her once again.

"Ugh!" Red's disgust with his ass was through the roof now as she stormed out of the office into a real storm ready to head to the bus stop.

She had only stepped a few feet from the door before Messiah's Beamer pulled up right along side of her. He was in the car with the same three guys she had seem him with yesterday. It was apparent that he never rode anywhere alone. As he rolled the window down staring at her being drenched in the pouring rain, all she could see was his pearly whites. Red looked down at herself then back up at him shrugging her shoulders then revealed a smile to counterattack his. Messiah shook his head at her intriguingly amused by the view.

"Where the hell are you going, girl?" He said as casual as could be. With his hand over his mouth shielding his laughter from her soaking wet nature.

"Your fucking gay ass helper wouldn't get you so I could interview for the job. He was too busy wrapped up in his ugly ass lover." Red said angry now that this was twice Messiah had seen her looking tore up.

Messiah's smile quickly turned upside down in a millisecond. He put the car in park and pushed the car door open hopping out leaving it running. He walked into the office followed by a soaked Red and stood there looking around at an empty office with a very pissed look on his face. He cut his eyes at Red then headed for the corner door banging on it hard like he was the police. The door flung open wildly revealing an angrily shocked Bently caught with his pants around his ankles this time. He quickly pulled his black slacks up tucking his elongated Johnson down inside.

"What the fuck is you doin' man?" Messiah snarled rubbing his finger across the bottom of his nose a few times.

CCUh, Meechie, I am so sorry. He just popped up over here and…"
Bently began stuffing his foot in his mouth as his companion slipped out the door straightening his flimsy gear.

CCMan, what the fuck I tell you about that shit at my establishment?
Let it happen again and your ass is out. Trust that. You got that big ass studio apartment upstairs and you wanna fuck in my business." Messiah scolded him as calm as ever. Red stood there with her arms folded loving the sweet taste of karma noticing Bently never looked up into either of their eyes not once.

CCBig Meech it will never happen again. I am so sorry. Please forgive me, sir." Bently finally cut his eyes at Red as she and Messiah headed out the door hand in hand.

She squinted her eyes at him and stuck out her tongue like a six-year-old child taunting him playfully. Bently shook his head in silence turning his lip up to her and sucking his teeth. He rolled his eyes and turned his attention out the window watching Messiah order his guy out of the front seat while Red slipped her wet ass inside. Messiah wasn't worried about ruining his Italian leather seats because material shit was nothing to him. It was the bread that was his concern. After he entered the car he pulled up to the gate and hit a button on his visor allowing the gate to click and slide open.

The row of storage units identically aligned all in a row looked worn like they had seen better days. But the huge pad locks attached to them let her know that they were as secure as a death row inmate strapped to the gurney. The lot had to be as big as

Midway Airport as they drove all the way to the back finally ending in front of a unit in the second row with no number on it. Red turned her head to the units on each side of the blank unit, 206 then 208 were there. But why hadn't 207 been placed there to identify the one they were standing in front of? She thought as she exited the car and stood in front of the unidentified unit closely attached to Messiah's hip. It seemed a little odd that they were there since she was supposed to be learning the ropes about the job. She hoped like hell they weren't about to gang rape her in a dirty ass storage unit.

Messiah's brother, Danger, hit the keypad on his Iphone then all of a sudden the unit's door clicked and began to rise. The men talked amongst themselves as the door clanged to the ceiling and they walked inside. There was absolutely nothing in the unit. Nothing at all it was even swept clean, but there was a big shiny rectangular object in the Far East corner. It appeared to have sliding doors but Red couldn't really tell from the darkness. They walked up on the object that was taller than them as Danger hit his keypad once more and the object opened. Red was expecting to see guns or something pop out but there was nothing but a silver empty box. Everyone entered and the doors closed. Red backed up from Messiah a little needing to keep her feet planted firmly on the ground just in case anything popped off, she was prepared to stand for hers.

The trip was short and sweet as the doors flung open revealing a long hallway with men posted along the walls. Every man had a Rottweiler by his side to accompany them in their security. All the men respected Messiah, giving him dap as they walked through the hall.

"Big Meech!" They yelled as he walked through like he was the king of a parade or something. It was something Red had never seen before but she loved the level of respect he was thrown and how the men seemed to bow to his every whim.

Red noticed that there were eight rooms aside the men with dogs made of huge glass paned floor to ceiling windows. It was very brightly lit in each of the rooms and they contained two or three half naked women each working on something at long black tables. There were no chairs to sit down anywhere and the women only wore white thongs with their tits flinging about freely. They wore pink flip-flop sandals on their feet and white paper masks over their mouths and noses. It was a very weird operation to Red not to mention how a simple ordinary storage unit could be so much more. Its look was more than deceiving but she didn't ask any questions. She thought it was best to keep quiet until she was spoken to so she could feel Messiah out and get an idea of why he wanted her to work there.

At the end of the hall was a big black door that swung open as another guy with a dog opened it for them.

"Alright. Everyone have a seat and let's get down to business." Messiah said pointing to a black leather chair in front of his huge ebony wood desk.

Red sat down never feeling something so warm, so smooth. She couldn't take her eyes off of the man of the hour wondering how he had become such an important man. Her heart fluttered like never before. She didn't think about fucking him or having his babies, none of that stupid shit women use to trap good quality men. She was thinking about falling in love with this man and making him fall for her. A man of his caliber should have a strong go-getter woman on his team and she wanted to be just that.

"Hey man, I gotta ride." Danger said flicking through his Iphone without looking up.

"Ah, the babes. Tell them I said whaddup." Messiah said shaking up with his brother and watching as he walked out the door never looking him in his eye.

First Day

Red stepped in Messiah's office right behind Skid, watching him closely as he handled business on the phone. He was a sight to see when he was at work. It was like watching the CEO of a major corporation conduct the day to day. Every time she was in his presence she felt light headed and dizzy like she would faint. It would have been nice to tell him how she felt but the fear of rejection seemed imminent. There was no way she was prepared to deal with that and she already knew what she needed to do to hook this dude real quick.

"Hey, there's my girl. You ready to work?" Messiah said smiling and standing to wrap his arms around her.

"Yep." Red responded shyly as she let him escort her out the door and into the hall or what was otherwise known as the "belly of the beast". She quickly whisked her white lab coat around onto her arms and straightened it as they walked towards one of the rooms.

"We have meetings in here everyday one hour before their shift starts. The chicks need to be kept in check, you feel me?" Messiah whispered into her ear so sweetly trembles shot through her body.

" Yes, baby." Red didn't mean to let that slip out that way but she was caught in the moment. Messiah looked at her and winked as he busted open the door like he was the SWAT team on a bust.

" Alright cease the chattering and get your asses in a seat." Messiah said walking to the front of what appeared to be a mock classroom full of scantily clad females and stood behind a metal podium. They all focused in on Red as she walked to the front of the room and stood a few feet behind him with her hands behind her back attempting to look innocent.

" First order of business, I feel like ya'll are taking my kindness for weakness. You're showing up late, not dressing in uniform when you come up in here. Ya'll know you supposed to be wearing the office work shirts. Don't come up in here looking like you fresh from the club. One more time and your ass is out. Period."

A few of the ten ladies in the back of the room began sucking their teeth giving fever to what Messiah had just spat. Red peeped the game and so did he but he wasn't in the mood to deal with catty females at this point, as he was ready to get back to his business in the office.

" Now you also know that payday is at the end of the month. So if it's not a dire need then don't come up in here talking about you need a loan so you can get your hair did. This ain't that type of establishment, ya heard." Messiah went on, as the cackling in the back of the room got a bit more disrespectful. He looked up out the top of his eyes and noticed the problem of the pack.

"Um, do you find something funny back there?" Red stepped in knowing Messiah wouldn't.

He was too soft on these bitches probably because they had been with him in the game for a minute or maybe he was fucking them. She didn't know and she didn't care but as long as she was running things they were going to have their asses in check.

"Who the fuck is this bitch?" A chick about the size of a NBA basketball player stood up with her saggy black tits swinging from left to right. Her weave was pulled back tightly in a bun and her nails looked like she swung from trees in the amazon some fucking where.

"Calm down Zadie, you need to watch your mouth alright?" Messiah stepped in extending his left arm letting Red know to call off the female breed inside of her.

"Naw, Big Meech. I'm not gone let whoever this is come in here and think she running shit. You just another bag bitch like the rest of us boo. Don't think you special just cause he about to introduce you." Zadie said rolling her eyes and crossing her legs as she sat down.

"Well if you must know, Zadie is it? I'm the new hall manager and when school is in session you need to get to class and don't be late. I'd hate for your mouth to sign a tardy slip that your ass can't cash, ya feel me?" Red snapped squinting her eyes devilishly at the girl as she returned the gesture.

"Shut the hell up! I don't wanna hear that shit. Y'all wanna fight take that shit to the streets but in here we doing business." Messiah roared.

When Messiah yelled it shut the whole room down, since he so rarely got angry at anything. Even the soldiers with their broad shoulders and funky attitudes in the back leaning against the wall were scared. Nobody had witnessed first hand the wrath of Messiah's anger but rumors and proof flirted around like wildfire of he and his brother's dealings in their younger days. The look on his face resembled the horrifying look Jack Nicholson had in the movie, The Shining. Everyone found themselves straightening up quickly before he unleashed the beast on them.

As the look slowly dissipated, he resumed his speech. "Now as I was leading up to, Red is going to be the manager around here. Any grievances you have or stock you need filled while on the job she will handle that for you. No one goes in the supply room at all, period. Is that clear?" He said clicking his teeth and licking his lips standing tall and confident, as a president should.

"Yes, sir." The ladies chanted in unison.

Zadie and her girls Tina and Marie, a pair of white girls from Oak Park who's parents cut them off financially so they had to work, were eyeing Red like a hawk on it's prey. They smiled casually as Messiah dismissed everyone not wanting to waste too much time on this shit and lose even more money than he already was. Red went and stood in the hall watching as the ladies filed into their respective workstations and began their work as usual. She looked over and noticed that one lady was moving a little slower than the rest and as she came closer to her she saw that she was pregnant.

"Hey, you alright girl?" Red asked as she walked up to her.

"Yeah, I'll be cool." The girl tried to walk around Red and continue on to her spot but she stood in her way blocking the path.

"Shit, you look like you about due huh? You might need to go home and get off your feet." Red said placing her hand on the girl's back. "What's your name?"

"Braze. But you don't need to help me I'm straight. You actually need to help yourself though." She said wobbling into one of the glass rooms.

"Why does everyone talk in code around here? What are you trying to say?" Red crossed her arms waiting on a response.

Braze turned around and stood up as straight as a board allowing her glowing perky brown nipples to point out like soldiers. She looked concerned down the hall wondering if anyone was listening then leaned in a bit towards Red's face.

"Look, don't pick a fight with Zadie, okay? She always gets her way and no one ever says anything to her. She will find a way to get you outta here. Just watch your ass."

Braze wobbled over to the table placing her paper mask on and getting right to work. She stood there waiting on Red to move along down the hall but she didn't. She was too preoccupied by Braze's words. But she was happy nonetheless to have received them since Braze didn't have to say anything and she did anyway. It was then that she decided she would keep her close to her side because that was the bitch she could trust.

****

"Why you play me in front of that ugly ass tramp, baby? I would have never done nothing like that to you?" Zadie said licking her lips and throwing her fat ass up on Messiah's lap.

"Hey, watch your mouth. She's not a tramp, she's my friend, and you will respect her just as you respect all the rest of my friends. Ya dig?"

Tina walked over enticed by her show and grabbed her ass pulling it up for him to get a better view as Zadie bent over. Marie stood there on shy mode wondering if she should get involved or leave. Embarrassed by her lack of balls to go over and join them, she just left the room to avoid any further humiliation. Tina bent over and sucked Zadie's ass cheeks loving the sweet and salty taste of her skin.

"Remember this daddy?" Tina asked Messiah as he stood there watching the show. "Remember me licking this pussy and making her scream your name?"

"You're nothing but a big tease, Tina. You don't give up no ass so who you frontin' for?" Messiah said trying to tame the beast within his pants.

Tina jumped up smacking Zadie on her ass as she stood up. "Well you loved it anyway." She said as she leaned in sucking face with him seductively.

She moved her tongue around in her mouth like a wild snake rubbing his dick through his pants trying to make it grow nice and hard.

"Grow for me daddy." She said tempting him into her seductive tricks.

Zadie cleared her throat loudly for Tina to get a handle on herself then she gave the signal for her to go on without her so she could have Messiah all to herself for a while.

Tina rubbed her C-cup nipples picking one up and turning it into her mouth then revealing her tongue slapping it on top. She smiled slyly as she hit the door and left the room. Zadie rolled her eyes pissed off and disgusted at that bitch always needing to have the center of attention just because she had a banging body and eleven percent body fat.

"Please leave." He ordered the horny on looking soldiers out of the room to attend to their duties.

They already knew what was going on and had been going on for long time but none of them cared. They just wanted a piece of that ass themselves but she wasn't biting. Zadie felt like she had the main man and that was all that mattered. She wanted to be his wife one day and be set for life by this man. She tried so desperately to get pregnant by him but Messiah was real careful, always slipping the condom on right before he stuck it in her. He was no fool.

"You need to learn to calm your little ass down, girl." Messiah said grabbing her wide ass bringing it in closer to him.

"I know baby but I don't like her. Why she gotta be here?" Zadie said in her elementary school girl voice. She always tried to butter him up with the voice and distract him with her body.

"It ain't about what you don't want. She's here to stay now deal with it." Messiah turned her around and began sucking on her dark brown skinned neck. He massaged over the tattoo of the words "Chocolate Thunder" on her inner thigh as he went to slip two fingers inside of her awaiting pussy. She moaned softly as his rough fingers mutilated her warm opening like it was punching through wood. He liked to keep it nice and rough with her no matter how much she said she hated it. She only wanted him to take it slow so it could feel like he was making love to her and he wasn't on that. There was only one woman in his life he would ever make love to and she wasn't her.

Zadie leaned her head on his shoulder loving every minute of his embrace and as she was imagining her two-car garage with a three-story house in the suburbs that she was working so hard to get, Messiah sharply pulled his fingers out and removed his shoulder making her head bobble like the doll. She was bewildered since he had never stopped in the middle of that shit before.

"What's wrong baby?" She asked rubbing his perfectly lined thin goatee.

"Nothing. We just ain't got time to play right now. We got work to do." He replied smelling the cherry scent of her pussy on his fingers feeling his manhood jump.

He was a sucker for the smell of woman's freshly scented pussy, but there was a time and place for everything and this was neither the time nor the place. Zadie grew increasingly angry, being riled up and not being able to get satisfied.

"Baby, that X ain't going nowhere. You know your girls gonna do whatever they got to so my baby can make his money." She went to him rubbing on his hard pecks hoping to get him back in the mood.

Messiah folded his arms and looked down at her like he wasn't playing. He didn't like thirsty women and that's exactly what she was acting like. He was a man who liked to take charge being very domineering and her whole desperate act for attention was a complete turn off.

" Meech, you got me fucked up if you think you about to leave me like this. Who you saving yourself for? Is it that bitch in the hall? Are you running up behind this bitch?" Zadie knew how to push Messiah's buttons and never liked to stop until he she saw the attitude on his face.

Messiah knew this but never let a bitch get under his skin especially a gold digging one. He looked at her with a smirk then straightened his suit jacket against his body and walked out the door. Zadie stood there pissed off as he left then fixed her thong and walked out headed for her post. He had never dismissed her like that so for him to do it was like a slap in the face. Red was walking back and forth checking on all the girls when she caught Zadie walking down the hall. She pretended not to see her and walked directly into her bumping into her shoulder with hers so hard that Zadie took a few steps backwards from the blow.

" You're late. Real late." Red taunted as Zadie stomped past her in a hurry trying to ignore her. Red was having a good time laughing in the process. "Awe what's wrong? Didn't get any daddy dick today?"

Zadie curled her lip up at her and rolled her eyes as she vanished into the room down the hall. Messiah openly crept out of the washroom drying his hands and looked down the hall at Red. He winked his eye at her making her blush as she turned around to get back to work. She wasn't about to abuse her blessing like Zadie and get lazy and unproductive. She knew she was a better chick than that beat up old bitch any day and one day Messiah would know that as well.

She couldn't understand what he saw in her in the first place. She was a tall ape like chick with a busted grill with the one tooth missing in front of her mouth and with all the money she made here it seemed like she couldn't keep her weave together. She had stretch marks on her ass, stomach, legs, and arms like she had been around the block a few times with a bus pass and a few kids and to top it all off she looked like she was damn near forty years old. Nonetheless she went to work just like the other girls for the five-hour haul.

****

Knock. Knock.

"I didn't mean to disturb you but it's 2am and all the girls are gone for the night so I'm locking up."

"Thanks, love. The days are long and vigorous here but it's the only way we all eat, you know what I'm saying? So did you like your first day?" Messiah leaned back in his chair and smiled.

"Of course I did. No complaints here."

Messiah smiled as she smiled. Every time he looked at her he felt some kind of way he couldn't explain. He knew she felt it too but they were both too caught up in their pride to express what they were feeling. Nevertheless, the emotion, fire, and passion was there. It was funny to him that she could come back into his life after all these years and make his heart flutter like she did when they were kids. He might have been a bit older than her then but she was more than just a kid then. She was his best friend and not even an age gap could prevent him from being soft on her. They stared at each other dreamingly for a few seconds before the silence was finally broken.

"Listen, Messiah. I just wanted to say thank you...for everything. I would still be on the streets if it weren't for you. Anyway, thanks." Red said attempting to leave out the door.

"Hey girl. Nobody works the shop on Fridays, you know that. So how about we make that a date? You know, to catch up and buy you some new clothes 'cause that shit you got on is through." He said as they both laughed at how true he was.

Red nodded her head in agreement. "I'd like that." She said as she closed the door and walked to the elevator.

She smiled to herself while getting on it but just as the doors were closing she noticed a tall shadowy figure standing in the distance. She couldn't make out who it was but she had a good feeling of who might've been. Red knew that Zadie was probably going to go in the office and suck Messiah off like a good little whore but she didn't care. She felt it was good for her to put in all the work she could because it would soon be all over once he was in her arms once and for all. She couldn't wait for the day that she would be able to watch her sitting in a corner looking shitty as she hugged and kissed on her man . It was defintiely going to be a world wind romance that Zadie could never experience but only visualize from the outside looking in.

2 Fridays Later

D rool crept out of Red's mouth making a gigantic puddle on her soft plush pillow. Pulling damn near all nighters every night at the Candy Shop was beginning to take a toll on her sleeping habits. She dreamt of the $5000 shopping spree Messiah had bestowed upon her two weeks ago. With all of the Fendi and Prada that surrounded her, she was truly a kid in a candy store that day and desperately yearned for another one. Her mouth was open and her eyes fluttered rapidly as she gradually entered the REM state of sleep and then there was a loud banging on the front door. She snorted up out of her slumber in a daze but highly upset at the disturbance. At first it seemed like it was all a dream since dead silence filled the room as she looked around for the cause of the sound. Just as she was about to choke it up as other people in the building, the banging returned.

CCWho the fuck is it? Come knocking on this damn door like you the fucking police. It better be Publisher's Clearing House with a huge check or somebody's ass is on the line." She snapped as she dragged slowly to the door whisking it open angrily so that whomever was behind the door knew she meant business.

"Well, it's your lucky day because I've got a big check." Messiah said waving a white envelope in her face. She smiled at the news quickly snatching the check out of his hand and clenching it to her chest. She rubbed it all over her body and under her arms loving every bit of her hard earned penny. Red wiped the drool from her mouth and tussled her hair in hopes that she hadn't looked so bad.

"Thanks! I can't believe it's the end of May already," she said kissing the envelope then slapping it down on the island counter centered in her kitchen, "but do you always deliver your employee's checks this early in the morning? Shit it's 8 am and I literally just went to sleep like five hours ago." Red said as went to the kitchen to make coffee and secretly stopped her ass cheeks from swallowing her shorts whole.

"Nope, just yours." Messiah looked around the condo loving the way she kept it immaculately clean as he plopped down on the sofa. He landed his arm right in the pillow drenched in drool. He raised his arm looking to see what was the moist substance lingering on it. Red raced over horribly embarrassed grabbing the pillow.

"Oh my gosh. I'm so sorry. I must've been sleeping harder than I thought." Red went to get him a towel from the washroom then returned to clean him off. She sat on her knees very close to him on the couch cleaning the wet patches of spit on his arm.

"It's all good, baby. It's just a little saliva." Messiah's eyes sparkled as they gazed into each other's eyes romantically.

There was just something about her that drew him in. He couldn't place his finger on it but whatever it was he liked the way it felt. He moved his arm around to her backside landing right on the top of her ass making sure not to grasp it fully. Red had gotten some weight back on her in the past few weeks, he noticed, as he pulled her in close to him. She was so close that she could feel his body temperature rise with every waiting moment. She could feel his breath slightly coat her cheek as he leaned his head to her ear wanting to nibble passionately on it but caressing the side of her face with his manly stubble instead.

Messiah moaned silently sounding like a purring tiger as he felt her smooth skin against his body. Her soft supple skin felt like it would melt like putty in his hands as her temperature now began to rise. Red's sexy feminine moan was just as soft, as she wrapped her arms around him inviting him into her warmth. The two rubbed each other's bodies, desperately needing, wanting more.

For the Love of Money, the Bone Thugs in Harmony song eroded from his jeans pocket loudly. Messiah dreaded answering, already knowing whom it was. He had assigned that ringtone for one person and one person only. He took the phone out of his pocket never batting an eye at it before he hit the button and put it to his ear.

"Hello?" He got up walking towards the door as if he was about to walk out.

Red was used to it. He was a busy businessman she got that aspect. There was no need for her to question his time since she knew she would see him soon. She returned to the kitchen hornier than a toad in heat, though, to retrieve the coffee from the maker. Just as she took a sip of the boiling hot drink from her mug, she was greeted with a hard schlong to her backside.

"When do you turn eighteen?" Messiah whispered into her ear seductively.

"Next week, June 7th." She closed her eyes leaning back into his strong embrace.

"Get at me then." He said slapping her on her ass mighty hard as he walked back towards the door. "Do something big, chick. Like a party or something, and don't worry about the dough, it's all on me. I'll come check you out." The door closed behind those words.

Red was elated bouncing up and down like a schoolgirl and displaying a smile like the Joker loving the fact that he was treating her with the utmost respect. She loved the restraint he exhibited even though it was clear they wanted each other bad as hell. Now all she had to do was get that nasty looking Zadie out of his life for good. She knew she had to keep her eyes open for any opportunity she could to axe that bitch out of his life for good and she knew just how to do it, catch that bitch stealing.

****

"You seem to be mighty chipper today. Did you get some pussy from your other little trick today? Let me guess, it was the one I saw in the condo over there on Harlem." Alexis said picking through her garden salad as Messiah took a seat at the table.

He sat there watching her with his hands folded on the table and a daunting look on his face. He wondered what the hell she was even doing at the condos since she never showed interest in wanting to do maintenance or even collect the rent from over there. The waiter made eye contact with him but he shooed him off. He waited for her to say anything else but she just kept stuffing her face so he decided to kick it off.

"We come to this expensive establishment every week, order the most expensive meals, drink the most expensive wine, and then when we're done we leave separately. You go back to your paid escorts and nothing changes. What's the point in doing this and marriage counseling if none of it is working?" He leaned forward to take a sip of the water from the wide wine glass. He pulled his suit jacket straight then checked his all white jumpers for any signs of dirt while dusting off his jeans.

"I think we both know what to call this." He said signaling the waiter for the check.

"No, Messiah, what do we call this? What I do is no different from what you do. You go to your ready made whores everyday and you expect me to believe you're not banging none of 'em?" She said sliding back a whole glass of Chateau Haut-Brion Blanc.

She sucked the food out of her teeth looking at him like she was hunting prey. She went back to her salad attacking it like animals on Animal Planet.

"Where you been all night, Alexis?" He asked calmly placing his finger to his lip and resting his head in his hand.

"I was at my sister's. Why?" She said stuffing her face.

The waiter brought her well-done steak and potatoes placing it next to her salad on the table then went around to the other side of her to pour her another glass of wine. Messiah signaled once again for the check figuring he may have forgotten as it was understandable. The restaurant was rather noisy for a brunch, busy for that time of morning, but at least no one could hear them arguing.

"You weren't there, Alexis, I know you weren't. I drove past there last night and I didn't see your truck." He said pouring himself a glass of wine.

"Why the fuck are you stalking me now? Don't you have other bitches to tend to?" She said carving a slice of her steak and stuffing it in her mouth closing her eyes in enjoyment.

"You started all this shit Lex. You haven't been faithful since the miscarriage. It's not my fault you can't have kids but I've never held that against you. Now look at you. A fucking X junkie. What keeps me with you, I'll never know. But I'm here and I'm trying to make this shit work…" Messiah said leaning in to touch her hand.

Alexis yanked it back before he got halfway across the table-cloth. "Make it work? Please. Yeah you fucking other bitches is really working for me. To tell you the truth you are wasting your money cause counseling is boring."

Alexis stuffed her face heavily like a raccoon but Messiah couldn't bring himself to say he wanted to let her go. She was his wife of four years and he wanted his marriage to work but if she wasn't willing anymore, there was nothing left for him to do but end it.

"Alexis, I love you…but I think it's time we split baby."

"Split what? Your money? 'Cause that's the only thing getting split if you divorce me bitch." Alexis said glugging down her final glass of wine and checking her Evo for the time. "File the papers and bring 'em to me. If you're ready to pay then I'll sign them, until then you'll have to excuse me. I have a date with Danger, you know your big brother right?" She stood plumping her 38C breasts her white tight fitting one shoulder dress and flipping her weave.

"Danger? Oh that's the reason why he ain't been to the shop in a few days, huh? 'Cause he's banging you." Messiah stood ready to slap her ass down to the ground right in the middle of the restaurant.

"Yeah, but what you don't know is that he's been banging this for way longer than a few days baby. I thought since we were being honest now, there was no need for me to keep hiding the shit anymore. So, when I'm out don't call my phone back to back like you've been doing. I'm busy. Okay hubby?" Amusingly blowing a kiss to him, Alexis snatched her snakeskin clutch off the table then rolled her eyes and pimped off feeling herself.

The waiter saw her leave and quickly shuffled to the table to finally hand Messiah the check. He looked down at the half eaten steak, barely touched potatoes and a smidgen of the thousand-dollar bottle of wine left. Alexis wasted money every chance she got. She found it funny to spend all of his hard earned money on bullshit because she knew he would always get more. She knew being broke was the root of all evil in his eyes and he would never subject himself to that.

Messiah sat down to finish the meal and wine while handing the waiter his Discover Card. Once he was done he dropped two hundred dollar bills on the table as a tip to the inattentive waiter and signed his government on the receipt then bounced.
****

"He knows baby, he finally knows!" Alexis exclaimed on her Evo driving frantically on the winding road as she left the restaurant.

"What does he know, Lex?" Danger asked seemingly out of breath.

"About us. He knows about us and ain't a damn thing he can do about it. His soft ass can't divorce me unless he gives up that cheddar. So we can be together out in the open now and we still got dough, baby." Alexis drove happily cheesing down the road. She was proud of herself having accomplished something not many women could claim.

"You shouldn't have done that Lex. You know I got things at home that ain't straight and you doing that just fucks things up between me and my little brother." Danger said.

"I thought that's what you wanted. You said you didn't care about him knowing about us now you bitching up on me?"

"Girl, call me back when you got that ass off them shoulders, ya heard?"

The dead silence crept through Alexis' soul like thieves in the night. She couldn't believe that he had treated her like this after all they shared together and she wasn't having it. She put the pedal to the metal as she raced for Danger's home on the East Side. She swerved through traffic luckily evading the law wanting to make it to his house before he tried to dip off. The engine roared on her 2011 Lincoln MKX, as the rage rose inside of her pulling up without parking in front of Danger's 2-flat building over looking the lake. She jumped out slamming the door and screaming at the top of her lungs, crazed and deranged.

"Danger! Get your punk ass out here!"

An otherwise lively neighborhood stood still trying to figure out whom this crazy chick was yelling like that and pulling out a bat from her trunk. Danger looked out the window in disbelief. Alexis had lost her damn mind and she showed no signs of gaining it back. He lowered his head shaking it hoping he would be able to diffuse the situation before it escalated.

"Who the fuck is that, D?" Amy asked.

"Nobody boo. Go back to sleep." Danger slipped his blue jean shorts on and then his all white Nikes leaving his bare breasted muscular chest to breathe.

He ran down the stairs swiftly running up to Alexis grabbing the bat in a game of tug of war, as she was about to swing on the taillights of his 2011 silver Dodge Charger.

"Bitch, is you crazy?" He asked breathing hard finally yanking the bat out of her hand.

"Bitch? Oh now it's bitch but last night it was baby." Alexis tugged on his shorts pulling him closer to her. "Why you actin' funny? Two years, Danger, and this is how you do me?" Her acting skills were superb, putting on the fake crocodile tears for Danger's sympathy.

"What is you talking about? I never said we was quits, you just trippin' too hard. You married girl, you need to stop this shit for real. Plus my baby mama is in the crib seeing all this…"

"Yo' baby mama? Like I give a fuck about her. My husband knows about you so why shouldn't she know about me, huh? This ain't nobody's business but yours and mine."

Just then Amy came wobbling her 6-month pregnant stomach out of the hallway.

"Danger, what's going on?" She asked flipping her long dirty blond hair to the back. She was a very quiet and subtle skinny white chick but piss her off and there would be hell to pay.

"Nothing baby, gone back in the house." Danger waved her off but she wasn't having that.

Clearly the chick he was talking to had some kind of beef with him and she wasn't leaving until she found out what it was. He turned back to Alexis hoping to reason with her but knew it would be damn near impossible.

"Look here, meet me tonight at our usual spot, Hard Rock, and we'll discuss this shit. I'm fucking begging you, man." The look in Danger's eyes was not of love or concern but of hatred.

He had already been going through relationship problems with Amy with her wanting to leave his cheating ass and that little spectacle wasn't helping one bit. He originally wanted to make Amy his wife and live the fairytale that his brother, Messiah was presumably living but it seemed like it would all be a dream if Alexis had anything to say about it.

"You'd better be there at 8pm or else I'm coming back and this time me and preggos over there will sit down and have a little talk." Alexis smirked as she walked off snatching her bat and tossing it back into her truck.

She winked at Amy as she got back into the car and pulled off wildly. Amy stood on the porch with her arms folded on top of her small tits with her lips curled up. This wasn't the first time some crazy broad had showed up at their spot ready to blow Danger's shit out of the water. But it was the first time he tried to reason with one. Amy wasn't stupid and Danger knew it. She was one of those females that gave you enough rope to hang yourself so that when you she left you it hit you harder than a ton of bricks. She knew Danger's conscience would eat away at him eventually with all the wrong doing he had done to her and her love for him wouldn't allow her to give up on him just yet.

"Not still fucking nobody, huh? I don't know why you keep fucking with me knowing what I'm capable of. Don't think just cause I'm pregnant that I'm vulnerable." She snapped all the way back into the house waddling the whole way.

Danger put his head down once more rubbing it roughly, thinking about all the times he had done her wrong. It wasn't that he didn't love her, it was that when he saw a fat ass or some nice plumped tits he couldn't control himself. But he never gave them his heart only his piece for a limited time. Alexis was the only one of his many women who ever caught feelings so tough. He was pissed off at himself for the fact that he may never get right with Amy at this point.

Happy Birthday

Red walked through the "belly" of the Candy Shop conducting business as usual. The girls were all working overtime so they could leave and go to her party at the Vertigo Sky Lounge at the Dana Hotel and Spa downtown. Quitting time was going to be a little early tonight for the elaborate affair that Messiah graciously funded. Zadie was even invited but of course not by her. She walked to the end of the "belly" to glance into the room she and her minions were working in. The soldier standing there, Pet, was on his cell phone chattering away with one of his many chicks of the night, inviting her to the party. He was so engrossed in his conversation that he barely saw her walk up. When he finally caught wind of her he knocked on the thick paned glass window pretending that the dog forced his hand back against it. The girls looked up noticing her white coat peeking around the corner and quickly returned their fingers to the table acting as if nothing was wrong.

It was just as she suspected. But she knew that she would need more proof then just her accusation. She huffed and laughed to herself knowing it was only a matter of time before this bitch fucked herself and now she had her right where she wanted her, caught with her panties down. Pet glanced at her as she walked back down the "belly" turning to look in the window at the girls giving them the nod that she was gone. As she made her way to Messiah's office she was halted and shocked by what she had seen through one of the windows. Braze had popped one of the pills in her mouth after she had finished putting it together. Red wanted to pretend like she didn't see it but it was hard to look away with her protruding belly staring her in the face. Braze looked up at her and smiled coyly acting as if she had done nothing at all.

"Messiah, can I talk to you for a minute?" She said knocking on his door and entering without waiting on him to invite her in. He looked up in dismay wondering if there was something wrong since she had never came in his office in the middle of a shift before.

"Yeah, whassup?" He said looking back down, writing on some papers on his desk.

"Have you ever thought about installing cameras in the rooms? I mean, then you could see first hand what's going on in those rooms you know." She said sitting down in the leather chair in front of his desk. He looked up smiling wondering where all of this was coming from.

"Well now if I did that, I wouldn't be able to see your pretty little face everyday now would I? 'Cause that's what I pay you for. Where's all this coming from anyway?" He said walking around to the front of the desk crossing his arms leaning in with interest.

"I just think that even though you have me to snitch on what's going on, you should still have the proof in the pudding you know what I mean?"

"It's funny you should mention that though. I already had them installed last weekend. So…what did you see?" He asked never dropping the smile from his face.

"Oh! Well, I'm sorry then you'll have your proof soon enough." Red stood attempting to walk out the door.

"Red," Messiah called after, "you still have a job to do."

"I just think you should watch the company you keep." She said slipping out the door.

He already knew whom she was talking about. He wasn't in the business of playing mind games and reading between the lines but he couldn't deny he had already felt the shit in his heart. He was broken as he turned on the 42" screen TV on the wall in front of him. He flicked to channel four displaying all the rooms in the Shop including the main office in full color. He watched as the ladies continued their work not seeing much going on. His eyes reflected upon Pet who was constantly tapping on the window alerting the ladies in the room to Red's presence. He sat back in the chair folding his hands and squinting his eyes.

"These young bastards don't know shit." He said angrily.

****

"Its time to go y'all let's get it!" Red said escorting the ladies out of her condo and into the waiting stretch party bus outside.

That bus was something out of a hip hop music video with two floors, a stripper pole running through the middle of it, a full open bar with personal bartender, and mirrors with disco lights streaming from the top. The DJ blasted music on the second floor as they danced on the first floor while the bus hit the road. The ladies were all laughing and having a blast drinking expensive champagne and feeling the cool breeze of the air conditioning against their faces. After about an hour of driving around downtown, the bus finally came to a halt.

"Everybody off the bus!" The bus driver announced over the intercom as he opened the doors revealing the beautiful hotel.

Red had never seen anything so beautiful. All of her years on the street and she had never even bothered to venture downtown. She didn't want to be reminded everyday of all the riches she could never afford. They stepped off the bus into the glass heaven and entered headed for the Vertigo. Red pulled her tight little skimpy halter red dress down as they trotted to the elevator in their red bottoms leaving all eyes on them.

The ladies were all smiles as they walked in the lounge in awe at the glamorous establishment. It was almost as dark as a nightclub inside but well lit enough that you could definitely see the outdoor fire pit from across the room. They hit the bar hard then ventured over to the VIP section ready to get their juke on, exclusively. Red danced her ass off happy to have finally made it not only off the streets but to see eighteen. Something she once thought was impossible with the life she was living. She paused her partying to thank the person who made it all possible. She wanted to lay a big juicy sloppy kiss on him right in front of Zadie so she would know she was being replaced and it wasn't a damn thing she could do about it. The very person who was responsible for helping to turn her life around for the better and give her things she would have otherwise only dreamt of having. But he wasn't there.

****

"Where the fuck are you going?" Alexis snapped as she fixed her makeup in the mirror preparing for another rendezvous with Danger.

"Does it matter? You're leaving so I'm doing me." Messiah stated as he slipped on his navy blue suit jacket and dusted off his Kenneth Cole dress shoes.

"I'm going with you." Alexis said grabbing her studded clutch off of her beauty desk.

She didn't really want to go but the way Messiah dismissed her pissed her off. He had never dared to talk to her like that and always worshipped the ground she walked on. She knew that he was trying to go out smelling and looking good with some fancy broad because he would get that snazzy for some regular trick.

"You're not invited." He said grabbing his keys and walking out of the bedroom.

"I don't give a shit. I'm going. If you prove to me that you ain't fucking around on me, I'll stop fucking around on you." Alexis crossed her fingers behind her back in her head.

She wasn't serious she just wanted to be nosey into his life and foil his plans for the night. He wasn't the one to go out much but ever since she had revealed her truth he has been finding reasons to get over her. He could only wish he could figure out how to get rid of her without losing everything that he worked so very hard for. Messiah waved her off allowing her to follow him to his car.

"So, which one of your bitches are we on our way to?" She taunted hoping to provoke a confession up out of him.

"Would you shut the fuck up? Damn, all you do is talk. You need to listen more than you open that whole in your face."

"Why should I listen to you? You're nothing but a little pussy who can't fuck! Yeah I said it! What a waste of a good size dick, too. I wonder if the little bitch you're fucking loves that shit." Alexis laughed.

SLAP!

"What the…" Messiah yelled. "Trick have you lost your damn mind hitting me in my face like that?"

"I beat your ass cause yous a punk! That's all you are. Ever since you got a little money you've just been soft. You used to want to fight over me and would snap if a fool looked at me wrong and now you don't do shit." Alexis let the visor down, checking her makeup once more.

"Estupido. Besa mi culo, puto!" Messiah only screamed in his language when he was highly pissed, as his foot pressed heavily on the gas revving the car up from thirty to sixty-five in under a minute.

"Don't talk that Spanish shit to me, jerk-off. Now stop the damn car! You ain't got the balls to be driving this damn fast!" Alexis tried to act like the speed wasn't scaring her but deep inside she was mortified. She had never seen this side of him before as she slowly began to realize she might have gone too far. Her taunting only fueled his anger even more prompting him to allow his foot to sleep on the gas pedal. Messiah turned his head eerily slow to her locking his eyes with her face. Then he blanked out unable to think clearly or say anything, the corner of his lips turned up showing every bit of his sinister looking smile. His eyes grew wider and wider and then all of a sudden there was a loud crunch and then silence.
****

"Happy Birthday!" Everyone yelled as Red blew out the candles shaped in the number 18. They toasted their champagne glasses in the air drunk but having an awesome time nonetheless. She was so happy that the night ended well with no drama or beef from anyone. Zadie was even cool even though she sat in the corner with her minions, Tina and Marie and was snickering with them all night. Red paid it no mind since she was patiently waiting for her secret love to arrive. It had already been three hours and the party was just about wrapping up as everyone was snatching their plates of the huge marble cake with whip cream icing and making B-Lines for the door. The party bus was outside waiting to drop everyone off at his or her destinations but Red wasn't ready to leave just yet. She still had faith that Messiah wouldn't stand her up like that. She knew he respected her too much to break her heart like that.

Zadie's cell phone began to ring and then Skid's rang right after. They both collided together to converse frantically about something immediately after. Red signaled for the bus to take all of the rest of the ladies home, as Braze was now fast asleep on the bus tuckered out from a long day.

"What's going on guys?" Red asked walking over to them as they walked outside together.

"Nothing you need to concern yourself with youngin'. Why don't you go home and call one of the little soldiers and get you some ass for your birthday?" Zadie's sarcasm struck a strong nerve with Red as her concern quickly turned into anger. She knew there was something going with Messiah and they knew it and she wasn't leaving until she found out what it was.

"Look you ape-looking trick. I don't care what our beef is but I need to know what is going on with Messiah. He's my fam and I ain't going nowhere until you tell me what's up."

Now aggravated at the level of maturity Zadie was displaying, Skid stepped in to end the issue. "Messiah and Alexis are at Christ Hospital, man. We need to get there like yesterday."

"Wait who's Alexis?" Red asked as Skid walked off towards his car not giving a shit if anyone followed him even though they did. They loaded up and took off into the night.

****

"So you're going to go to the hospital to see if that bitch is okay?" Amy said slapping clothes down unto the bed for her to get dressed. "Then I'm going too."

"Whoa! You ain't going nowhere with my son inside you girl. Chill out, I told you my brother was in that car too man. It's not about her. I don't care about her. I want you, babe, I wanna marry you." Danger said grabbing his wallet off the nightstand.

"You wanna marry me but you fuck other bitches from time to time and I'm supposed to be okay with that? Just because I'm white, Danger, don't mean you can fuck me over fool. I'm white, not stupid." Amy said sitting back against the headboard of the bed.

"Who said anything about you being stupid, boo? You being white has nothing to do with it."

"Yes it does, Danger. Cause you go out there and do what you want and you figure that just because I'm white that I'm naïve and I'm going to stick with you regardless and…"

Danger looked at her crazy believing that she definitely watched too much damn TV.

"Hol' up, hol' up. Baby you going off the deep end. It's just your hormones. I don't think any of those things about you Amy. I love you and I respect you. You got my seed and you most definitely gone be my wife. I just need to get some things in order first."

"Things like what? Like quitting your sideline hoe?" Amy said crossing her arms.

Danger kneeled down by her side rubbing her stomach with his huge rough hands.

"Babe, fuck her. I only want you and as soon as that bitch drops me this connect to the product we gone. How else am I going to give you the wedding of your dreams?" He kissed her hand and stomach gently then raced out the door.

Amy knew he was feeding her bullshit but she felt it was nice to have a man that cared enough about her to want to try. Besides there was no way she was raising his son on her own.

"Ayo, Meech. You okay man?" Danger said answering his Iphone as he put the car in drive and pulled off. "I'm on my way to you right now."

"How'd you here about the shit, dude?" Messiah whispered.

"Man, dude that shit was bad as hell on the e-way. It's on the news and er'thing kid. I called Skid and told him to bounce over there."

"Oh…alright then."

"Ayo, Meech man, whatever that chick told you man, it ain't true. You hear me, dude? It ain't true." Danger heard nothing but the silence of the cold phone to his ear. Messiah had hung up on him not wanting to hear any bullshit that was about to fly out of his mouth.

****

"Oh my God! Meech are you okay pookie?" Zadie rushed over to hug and kiss all on his cheeks and neck. He slapped hands with Skid giving each other a tightly knit handshake then dispersing as they normally did. Skid posted up just close enough for him to hear Messiah if he needed him. He brushed Zadie off peeling her clingy arms from around his neck and made his way over to a waiting Red leaned against the wall.

"Did you have a good time at your party tonight?" He asked looking down at her displaying a coy like demeanor. She wanted to bombard him with questions but knew that would only be a turn off so she decided to keep it cool and sweet.

"Yeah, it was nice. It was just missing one thing, though." She said looking up into his big brown eyes counterattacking its charm with her pearly white smile.

Zadie stood there with her arms folded and one leg extended furiously. She couldn't believe this fool had played her after everything they'd shared together.

She cleared her throat. "Um, Messiah. Don't you see me standing right here?"

"Yeah, I said wassup." He said never taking his eyes off of Red.

He loved the way her red birthday dress was wearing her. All he could think about was tearing it off and watching her walk around in her high-heeled stilettos.

"Messiah Torres." The white-coated doctor came out from around the corner looking around for him.

He raised his finger indicating his presence then walked over grabbing Red's hand to come with him.

"Mr. Torres, your minor cuts and bruises are going to be fine but you may experience some swelling within the next couple of days. Sometimes people's bodies go into a bit of shock from being thrown around so roughly. You'll be fine, though. This prescription should take care of all of that." The doctor handed Messiah a square like blue slip of paper.

"Alright thanks doc, and uh, what about my wife?" Messiah asked feeling Red try to slip her hand from his in disbelief. Wife? She thought as she stood there trying to slow her breathing from the initial shock.

"Well right now she's still unconscious and it's pretty touch and go at this point. We'll keep an eye on her just in case anything changes."

"But she's gonna be okay, right?"

"Well…right now it's not looking good. Get some sleep, son. You're gonna need it." The doctor walked off in the opposite direction from whist he came.

"Meech?" Zadie bellowed again but he pretended he didn't hear her.

He focused in on his brother walking through the emergency room doors dreading every minute he stared into his face. He was his brother and he loved him but he was living foul. he only called him to let him know that he was good before he heard it from anyone else. Despite everything, they were brothers and it was blood to the end with them. But he knew all Danger would do was continuously apologize to him, plead his case, and lie about his affair with Alexis and he just didn't feel like hearing that shit right then.

"Skid!" He yelled waving his two fingers in his brother's direction.

Skid already knew the drill. He interrupted Danger's path to him as he and Red slipped out the door on the other side of the nurse's station. Zadie watched in agony as her love and her money walked out the door leaving her behind. Skid let Danger know that Messiah wasn't seeing anyone tonight in a not so friendly way then walked out the door to meet him at his car. Heated, Danger walked slowly up to Zadie realizing her facial expression looked the same as his. Even though they never got along, he wanted to know what was going on with his brother. He didn't know why his brother was being anti-social at a time like this but he reluctantly walked over to get the 411 from her.

Cut Off

"Well that's one hell of a birthday present to give me." Red snapped as she entered her condo and threw the keys on the coffee table.

Messiah smirked as he lowered his head unwilling to go through the motions with yet another female, especially not right then.

"Listen, I didn't tell you about her because it was on a need to know basis. You didn't need to know because right now she's irrelevant."

"Irrelevant? Irrelevant? She's your wife, Messiah. Your fucking wife! That's about as relevant as they come don't you think?" Red was irate. She was so glad she hadn't slept with this fool before she found out that detail. Having a girlfriend was one thing but a wife was a long-term commitment that he had made to someone pledging his undying love. She always thought she would be that special person someday but all of that was quickly stripped away.

"Woman, calm down. We going through some problems alright. She cheating and disrespecting me and shit. It's crazy. Look I don't wanna talk about her alright." Messiah leaned back on the couch with his head facing the ceiling.

He closed his eyes to finally feel rested and at peace. Red watched as the exhausted man lay back trying to get comfortable, fidgeting to get a groove in the couch.

"Come on." She said tugging on his Incredible Hulk hand.

He got up following her to the back bedroom and landed face first unto the plush pillow set atop of her huge king size canopy bed. She removed his shoes for him then unzipped her red dress removing it right in front of him. Messiah glanced out the corner of his eye at her undressing once he heard her zipper become undone.

"Get over here girl." He said licking his lips like he was about to sop her up with a biscuit.

She walked over to her all white dresser with gold trimming opening the drawer to pull out the silk blue night gown he had brought her a few weeks ago, his favorite color. When he saw it he knew he was in. Even though his body was beginning to lock up just like the doctor stated, he was going to get her ass one way or the other. She slipped on the nighty with ease then made her way over to the bed walking seductively and laid in his arms.

"Good night." She said as she gathered her pillows fluffing them up before plopping her head on them.

Red moved her body like a snake to get underneath the covers then turned her back to Messiah staring out of the window. She smiled a little inside punishing him for not telling her about his wife but she hoped her little game hadn't pushed him away entirely. Just as she was closing her eyes drifting off to sleep she felt his large body surround her like an ocean current. He leaned in and squeezed tightly kissing her forehead in the process.

"I will get you," he whispered, "but you can be mad tonight." Red scooted over towards his cuff allowing him to squeeze her even tighter as the couple drifted into a deep slumber.

The next morning, Red found herself in bed alone. She rose and went into the living room to see if he was there and turned looking at the kitchen but there was no one. He had left her alone. She could still feel the sweet caress of his touch on her body. Though she played the fool last night she desired some early morning action. Her plan was undoubtedly foiled by his disappearing act and there was no sign of a note or message. She leaned against the living room window gazing out unto the brightly sunned neighborhood remembering his words of his marriage being in trouble. She figured whether Alexis lived or died, Messiah's heart was hers. She daydreamed of their night together and hoped she would have another shot at his love later.

****

"Alright doc, I'll be up there in a few minutes." Messiah said slamming down the phone.

phone out of her bra punching the keys wildly.

"Can you believe this fool just quit me?" She yelled into the phone walking back to the gate.

She signaled for Bently to buzz her out as she rambled on about how Messiah played her so bogus. She walked on top of the grass dodging light poles along the way heading towards the Target parking lot behind the Shop. Just as she had reached her brand new 2012 Mazda CX-9 that she had been hiding from Messiah for the last 6 months, an unmarked car pulled up on the side of her really quickly. Out jumped to detectives flashing their shiny silver badges in her face before they spoke.

"Zadie Atterberry?" One of the men said walking on the side of her ensuring to secure her in a box so she couldn't flee the scene.

Zadie looked at both of them inquisitively wondering what the hell they might have wanted with her.

"Marie, let me call you back girl." She said hanging up the phone and stuffing it back down in her bra. "Who wants to know?"

"I'm Agent Crosby and this is my partner Agent Maxwell, DEA. We just have a few questions for you and we'd like you to come on down to our office and talk about it." Agent Crosby said placing his badge back on the side of his hip. "Am I under arrest?" She asked placing her hands on her hip, sassy-like.

"No, but we..." Agent Maxwell tried to say but was cut short.

"Then this conversation is over." Zadie said attempting to grab her car door handle but Agent Maxwell put his hand on it preventing it from opening.

"Listen, gal. We don't want you. We already know who you are and what you do. We want your little boyfriend, Messiah Torres. He's in some mighty big bullshit and if you don't help us out you're going down with him." Agent Maxwell smiled at her sure of himself that he had her right where he wanted her.

"You don't scare me. I know how you overachieving cops are. Always sending checks you can't possibly cash without someone's signature. If you'll excuse me gentlemen, I have prior engagements." Zadie said yanking the door open with Agent Maxwell's hand still on it.

"Okay, okay we don't want any problems here. So, if you change your mind and want to talk to us, don't hesitate to give us a call." Agent Crosby said reaching in his pocket and pulling out a business card to hand to her.

She didn't want to take it at first but it seemed they wouldn't stop with their relentless antics until she did. She snatched the card out of Crosby's hand and got in the car slamming the door behind her. They stood there watching as she started up the car and pulled off hoping to have gotten through to her. She was their only hope of infiltrating the Candy Shop and getting the play by play of what goes inside. Everyone else they had tried to get a hold of wasn't talking or evaded their visits. The two agents got in their dark blue unmarked car a bit disappointed at the lack of results and drove off. Bently stood there looking out the window in shock that the feds were closing in on Zadie. He knew eventually she would crack cause her mouth was like a broken leaky faucet, always running. He picked up the phone immediately to run his.

****

Messiah rubbed on her freshly shaved smooth legs enjoying the softness under his hand. He couldn't think of a better place to be then right there laying with Red. She was everything he had looked for in a woman. She was caring, considerate, and classy and didn't nag him. Messiah was most attracted to the fact that she let a man be a man. Red giggled as he laid his head on her lap tickling her with his beard. She stroked his head gently as he closed his eyes and imagined her as his wife. He thought about enjoying her on the balcony of the hotel in Barbados overlooking the ocean as the sunset illuminated their bodies instead of the bickering that went on when he took Alexis there.

" I'm glad you came back baby." She said enjoying his weight on her body.

" Yeah, I like being here up under you. I wish I didn't have to leave."

" So don't."

Messiah cleared his throat, relieving the frog that was stuck in it. "I have to go to the hospital and check on Alexis."

"You know, you could've told me about her. It would've been cool. I mean after all we don't have anything going on…right?" The words came out of her mouth uncontrollably. She wanted to know exactly what was going on between them but she didn't want to seem pushy. She could feel the chemistry between them but for some reason she needed the reassurance that what she was feeling was real and not fantasy.

"I know. I just didn't want you to blow me off."

"You know…I'm not as innocent as you may think I am, Messiah."

"Who said I thought you was innocent?"

The couple chuckled as he tickled her stomach in a rough playful motion. He pulled her legs down bringing her directly under him. He was mounted on top of her looking down into her beautiful hazel bronzed skin and her dark chocolate hair. Her eyes batted at him waiting for him to finally make his move, sparkling up at him. He felt mesmerized by beauty never wanting to take his eyes off of her. He leaned in closely touching his nose with hers and Eskimo kissing her smiling the whole time. She thought it was cute that he seduced her in an entirely different way then she was otherwise familiar with. It felt damn good. It felt almost like love but with all of the wrong in her life it was hard for her to be sure.

"Kiss me already." She said deflecting the attention from her nervousness of him being so close.

H e planted his lips on hers kissing her passionately, rolling his tongue around with hers. She moaned softly as they became more engaged in each other. He stroked her hair pulling it loving the fact that it was all real, no tracks. She rubbed on his broad shoulders loving his bulge and reaching under his white t-shirt to get a better feel. He moved his hand downward to her soft breasts rubbing gently loving her velvety plumpness. Red's pussy throbbed with moisture as he placed his manhood against her loveliness raising her legs in the air. Their clothes felt constricting as their bodies danced together on the bed.

A t the same damn time, at the same damn time...

M essiah's phone rang interrupting the flow but he was ignoring it unconcerned with its presence. He continued his lustful acts moving down to her neck sucking and nibbling but careful not to suck to hard to leave any unwanted marks. Red tried to ignore it as well since she wanted this so badly but it was hard to concentrate with the phone ringing back to back.

"Just answer it babe." She finally gritted her teeth to say.

G runting irritably, Messiah yanked the phone from his jeans and answered it.

"Hello?"

"Yes, Mr. Torres. I was just calling to let you know there is no change in your wife's brain activity so that part is fine but she is still in a coma. However, she appears to be in a considerable amount of pain. So I'm calling to find out if it is okay to up her pain meds." The doctor said.

"Oh, uh, yeah. It's okay."

"Yeah, the rules have changed now and so we need the permission of the family in order to do so. That's all."

Messiah wasn't the least bit interested in what the doctor was talking about. It seemed he was looking to have casual small talk but as the phone grew silent he finally gave up and ended the call. Red continued to kiss him without any questions. She didn't care about the business he had to handle she was just finally ready to feel him inside of her. She felt him resisting the need to feel her, touch her, or hold her. She immediately stopped her lusting. She didn't want it if his heart wasn't in it.

"What's wrong?" She asked.

"Nothing...I just feel bad." Messiah replied looking deep into her eyes feeling her empathy for his problems.

"I'm listening."

"Nothing, nothing. Hey, can you come somewhere with me?" He said rising to straighten the now limp Johnson in his pants.

"Anywhere."

"I need to eat some Italian food. It always makes me feel better."

Red thought it was the weirdest thing for him to say since her opening was humming like a hummingbird. "Uh, yeah. Let's grab some grub!" She said lively trying to pep him up.

He had to admit, she made him smile.

Served Cold

Danger slowed the car down pulling up in front of Lake Michigan in the parking lot of Rainbow Beach. He took the joint from the ashtray and lit taking a few puffs then passing it to Zadie. She took a few long drags when Danger slapped her hand damn near knocking it out. She gave him the look of death as she slowly handed it back to him.

"So that dude dropped you like a bad habit last week, huh?" Danger asked.

"Shut up. He did not drop me…I ended it."

"Yeah, whatever you need to tell yourself. So anyway, what do you want from me?"

"Since I'm fired, I can't even get past the gate anymore. But you can. All I need you to do is lure that little bitch from the Shop Thursday night and drop her off on 119th at that old warehouse. I'll take care of the rest." Zadie said turning to look Danger dead in the face letting him know she wasn't playing.

"What? Girl you crazy. From what I hear Skid drives her everywhere so how am I gonna pull that off?"

"I don't give a fuck how you pull it off just do it. I promise you will be rewarded handsomely."

"Zadie, even if I was to pull the shit off, what's in it for me?"

"You've always wanted to get out of your brother's shadow and be in the limelight, right? So this is your chance. We'll frame him for her murder and you can have all the access to the merch and his money."

The sound of him finally being the top dog in the operation sounded really good to Danger. Ever since he started sleeping with Alexis he found himself at the office less and less unable to face his brother knowing he had just had his wife. But Messiah would never give him any real responsibility anyway, which pissed him off to the fullest and made him too lazy to even want to go into the office.

"Besides, I have proof that the feds are closing in on him. So once he goes down for this murder he'll go down for the X as well." Zadie laughed.

"Murder? Why are you doing this? I thought you loved that fool?" Danger asked flicking the duct out the window at some pigeons.

Zadie sensed some hesitation on Danger's part. She knew he needed more persuasion but she wasn't trying to sleep with her man's brother just to do it. She wasn't concerned about him telling his brother about her plan due to the bad blood between them so in that instance she decided to choose a different subtler route. As the car grew silent, Zadie took out her phone and began texting someone she knew was down for her offering him the same deal.

"I do love him but he needs to pay for what he's done to me."

****

Messiah sat in the chair of the hospital room watching Alexis lay perfectly still in the bed. She was wrapped neatly in the sheets and had tubes galore coming from her mouth and arms. He folded his hands and rested his chin upon them as he stared at her. His heart was heavy knowing he had put her there and there was nothing he could do to change it. He only wondered what might be going on if she wasn't in this predicament and then he remembered she hated his guts. He never knew what he did to deserve such hatred and even if she were conscious she would never tell him. Still she was his wife and he couldn't get past his love for her. He was truly torn between a love he knew was real and the woman who once was about to bear his child.

"Mr. Torres. I'm glad you're here. I have some papers here for you.

It's been about a week now since the accident and your wife's condition remains the same. My question to you is a difficult one. Do you want to continue with life support or do you feel the need to terminate?"

"Terminate? You're asking me to kill my wife?"

"Well we don't like to use that term but technically...yes." The doctor stood as cold and stiff as a tree on a winter morning. He was truly emotionless and he had to be since he dealt with this kind of thing on an everyday basis.

"You want me to give my consent to terminate my wife like she's a broken computer or something?"

"Yes that's the idea."

It took all of messiah's might not to slap the dog shit out of the doctor right then.

"I'm not signing that shit doc. Her blood will not be on my hands, no."

"Son, I know you're having a hard time dealing with this. Any human would in this case. But you've got to start thinking about the quality of life she's going to have remaining in a hospital bed in a vegetative state for how ever long it takes for you to get over the fact that she's gone." The doctor put his hand on Messiah's shoulder then walked out the room.

Messiah walked over to the window staring out unto the city. It was so beautiful from up there; it looked as if he was looking down on everyone from heaven. Just as he was about to allow a single tear to fall from his eye, Agent Crosby and Maxwell came walking through the door with flowers. Messiah couldn't pretend he didn't know who they were. They gave off the stench of moldy old swine.

"Gentlemen, what can I do for you?" He asked sitting back down in the seat crossing his legs and hands.

"Well, we heard that your wife here was in a little accident and uh, well, we decided to pay our respects." Agent Crosby said placing the flowers on the desk near the bed Alexis lay in.

"Did you?"

"Yeah I mean, why else would we be here?"

Messiah noticed Crosby give Maxwell a signal then Maxwell went and stood on the outside of the door making sure nobody came in.

"So, Mr. Torres, or should I call you Big Meech? You know for someone to have a name like Big Meech you've got to be doing some big big things. So what kind of things do you do?"

"I work. You know my business. I work that's it. You need my tax returns go get 'em. You know where they're at."

"You're wasting my time, Mr. Torres, just tell me what I want to hear."

"Listen, Mr..." Messiah paused.

"Crosby."

"Right. I don't know what you're looking for but whatever it is, I can assure you, you're barking up the wrong tree here."

"Here's my card. If you so happen to change your mind let me know. Maybe I'll cut you a sweet deal."

The men darted eyes at each other as the agent turned to walk away. "Oh and uh, give your wife here my regards."

The agent walked out of the door leaving Messiah with his thoughts. He already knew what the son of bitch wanted. He wanted a hand out just like the rest of them. But Messiah wasn't about to give in to some low level DEA agent on a power trip, struggling to pay his mortgage. Those cops didn't scare him the least bit. He had bigger concerns and it started with his wife. He didn't know what he was going to do if she died but one thing was very clear. He couldn't cheat on her anymore with anyone.

Messiah felt in his heart that when she woke up she would be a totally different person and would want their marriage to work. She was the only woman who stood by him when times were rough and he felt that all of her drug and alcohol abuse and cheating was only her lashing out at the fact that she lost the baby. Messiah was determined to stand by his woman come hell or high

water. He needed to be there for her in every way that a husband should. Even if that meant concealing his weakness for Red.
****

R ed knew something was wrong. Messiah hadn't been to the office in days and he wasn't answering his cell phone either. She wondered what was wrong with him or if he was even okay. She walked the belly of the beast not even paying attention to any of the girls in the room. They could have walked out with the whole supply and she wouldn't have even noticed. Her heart was breaking not knowing what was up with Messiah.

"So, you know today's my last day, right?" Braze said waddling out of the room headed for the washroom.

"Wow, It's been that long already?"

"Yeah girl, I should be popping this one out any minute now. Shit I hope sooner than later, ya know. So, why the long face?"

"Braze, you wouldn't understand."

"Try me while you help me to the washroom." The ladies chuckled as they slowly crept down the hall.

"Have you ever felt like you were so in love with someone that you would do anything for them but you didn't know if they felt the same way?" Red asked.

"Everyday. So who is he? You can tell me." Braze had a feeling she already knew the answer.

Red smacked her lips at her knowing that she barely knew her but she was all she had to confide in at that moment.

"It's Messiah. I know we've only been back in each other's lives a short time but I really feel close to him. Like there's nobody else in the world but me and him."

"Hm. Big Meech, huh? What do you mean back in each other's lives?"

"He used to babysit me when we were younger."

"Oh that's right you're still a baby aren't you? Sweet little Red, still has more growing up to do." Braze snarled sarcastically as she continued to waddle down the hall.

"Okay what the hell does that mean? I thought you was my girl?"

"Things change. Meanwhile, we barely know each other. How could you think we were friends?"

"Because I watched you pop pills every night in those rooms and you're fucking pregnant. But I never say anything cause it's your business."

"You're fucking right it's my business you little whore. And I warn you not to get in my business." Braze said pimping off.

"What's your deal? You just flipped the script on me in less than ten seconds." Red yelled after her but it was no use.

THUD! Red heard as she turned her head trying to forget about what was just said. She doubled back and saw Braze laid out on the floor. She rushed over to her instantly and lifted her head. Her heart was beating a mile a minute unsure of what the hell to do and afraid to call 911.

"Braze what happened?"

"I slipped on my water. It broke as I was walking."

Red looked down at the dry floor wondering what the hell she was talking about but was distracted by Braze's ratchet screams. She laid there holding her stomach as if she was about to go into labor. Red didn't know the first thing about birthing babies and prayed she could hold it in until she figure out how to get her help.

"Oh my God. Skid! Skid!" Red yelled out to the office where Skid jumped up out of his nap.

"What the fuck is going on out here?" Skid said looking like the devil had taken over his soul.

"Braze needs to get to a hospital fast. She's in labor."

"Damn, man! I'm not supposed to leave the Shop."

"Fool go!! This shit is a very serious emergency. I got this and I'm sure he will understand."

"Alright, alright."

Skid picked Braze up off the floor like he was scooping up kitty litter and raced towards the elevator. All of the girls were cheering for her as they disappeared into it then slowly filed back into their rooms. Red felt as if handling the lockup of the Shop would be a breeze. She went into the office and cut the lights off not feeling the need for anyone to go in there and when she came out Pet knocked her in the head with the back of his 9mm. Red was helpless as her body was dragged all the way to the elevator and left there.

Tina and Marie escorted the rest of the girls out of the Shop with guns to their heads threatening death if they opened their mouths about this to anyone. Tina snatched Red's phone using it to open and close the storage door letting the other girls out. Pet had promised the rest of the soldiers a cut if they agreed to help, which they inevitably did with their greed taking over. They cleaned out Messiah's whole supply of X, taking the capsules and ransacking his office looking for a way into the safe. They hadn't much time since Skid would be back any minute but they were prepared to stretch his ass out if they needed to.

"How the fuck do you get in it?" Pet said scrambling to look for a keypad or something to crack the safe.

"Shit I don't know I've never been in here." Tina said looking around the safe.

"Fuck that safe. We got the merch so we need to bounce." Marie said heading to the elevator.

Everyone quickly followed on the same page as she and ran down the hall. Pet handed his black bag containing a portion of the merch to one of his boys as he picked Red up and threw her over his shoulder entering the elevator. Outside they loaded up in the soldier's two company black Expeditions packed like rats and road out. Pet hit the gate giving the signal to Bentley to open it acting as if everything was cool. The windows were tinted so black that he couldn't see inside of them but he buzzed the gate and allowed them to drive through. Bentley looked up at the clock on the wall and realized they were leaving the Shop early tonight. There were plenty of times Messiah would give everyone time off so he thought nothing of it and made sure they were gone before buzzing the gate back closed.

"Baby don't stop they're gone now." Bentley said with his elbows resting on the desk and leaning his head back in enjoyment.

This time he had a Spanish fruit topping in the office giving him one of the greatest blowjobs he'd ever had in his entire life. That fool read his body like an open book as his legs trembled with excitement. He was so engaged in the feel of the man's mouth around his scrawny charcoal colored schlong that he hadn't even focused on the two men entering the office. One of the men took out his cop issued Glock 23 and pointed it at Bentley's head hoping that would get his attention, but it didn't.

"Ooo, baby I'm bout to bust!" Bentley moaned.

"And so am I." Agent Crosby said.

Startled, Bentley turned around becoming face to face with the barrel of the gun and now shaking for an entirely different reason. His man friend rose slowly wondering what the hell was going on and putting his hands in the air.

"Don't shoot please." He recited as he wiped the slob from his lips.

"What can I do for you?" Bentley asked never taking his eyes off the gun.

"Looking for Messiah Torres. I know he's here and I know the drugs are here. So point me in the direction of them and nobody gets hurt." Crosby said.

Bentley looked at his partner, Maxwell, who was just standing there with his arms folded smacking his gum like it was going out of style. Both of them had on their bulletproof vests but they would be no match for the huge stinger he had laying no less than a few inches from him under the desk. He wanted to reach for it but he thought about how wise it would be for him to have two dead cops in the office and how much more trouble it would bring Messiah.

"He's not here. I would suggest you come back during normal business hours." Bentley said sarcastically.

"Do I look like I'm fucking amused here? Where the fucks the drugs?" Crosby became irate moving closer to Bentley's face.

His friend had become hysterical, crying and waving his hands in front of his face wildly. Crosby grew annoyed from it all and pointed the gun at him. "Shut the fuck up!" he yelled.

"I don't know where any of that stuff is dude. All I know…"

"Yes…what is it?"

"I know that if I did know anything I wouldn't tell your cracker ass shit!" Bentley stood there waiting for them to jump hard.

They agents laughed hysterically realizing that these fools had no idea who they were dealing with.

"So, you boys like to take it in the ass huh? I bet you don't know what a real dick looks like. Get the keys to that storage unit right there." Crosby said putting his weapon down by his side still clenching it.

Bentley knew that these assholes weren't right the minute he set eyes on them. He honestly never knew how to get in the Candy Shop and for that matter really didn't know what took place down there. All he knew was how they got in and out, that was it. But it seemed that he and his friend were about to pay for the shit he didn't know.

Caught Up

"Girl, you better be lucky you pregnant, else I'd kick your ass dead in your mouth." Skid said walking back to the car.

"I'm sorry. How was I supposed to know that I wasn't in labor? This is my first kid you know." Braze said opening the car door tugging at the huge jogging suit Skid had given her to put on, on their way to the hospital.

"You fucking with my money now with all this shit."

"Um, can you just drop me off at home? I'm not feeling well."

"Hell naw. You about to choke it up and take your ass back to work. You gonna have to work overtime to make up for this shit."

Braze became worried. She didn't want to go back there at all and they assured her that this would all go according to plan. She started to hyperventilate, scooting down in the seat and cocking her legs open letting all of her funk out.

"Damn girl, what the fuck is wrong with you? Close that shit up and quit acting. You fucked up once tonight don't make it happen again. I will slap a bitch." Skid said covering his nose and becoming increasingly angry at her show.

When Braze realized that her lies weren't working, she decided that desperate times called for desperate measures. She started kicking and screaming and pulling on the seat belts and steering wheel almost causing Skid to swerve off the road. Before he knew it he had reached up and slapped her right in the mouth.

"What the hell are you doing? You trying to kill us or something? Now move again and see won't I slap your ass again. I told you I'm not scared to slap a bitch." Skid said now pulling into the driveway of the Candy Shop.

He looked over noticing Bentley was gone and just assumed he had gone upstairs for the night. He hit the button on his visor watching as the gate slid to the right. He drove like a bat out of hell to the entrance to the underground then tugged Braze on her arm, as she cried hysterically not wanting to go inside. She cried all the way to the bottom floor as the doors opened revealing an empty shop. Skid looked around in shock clueless as to what the hell happened. The dogs were roaming freely wondering where everyone was themselves, as Skid dragged her to the office to make sure everything was still there. He looked at her shaking his head then slapped her again. She curled up in the office couch holding her face and her stomach at the same time.

"What happened?" Skid said grinning evilly.

"I don't know what you're talking about." Braze lied.

Skid reached his large hand up again ready to knock her teeth out of her mouth if she lied again. "What happened? Did that little bitch, Red have something to do with this?"

"No, no, no." She shivered on the couch shielding her face from another blow.

"You've got five seconds to tell me what happened or I'mma knock that baby out of your ass. Five, four, three…"

"Okay! Okay! They gonna kill me, man…"

"You don't need to be worried about them you need to be worried about me right now." Skid said grabbing her up by her arms then throwing her back down on the couch.

"It was Zadie and Pet. They said to stage this shit and it would be so easy. They said no one would get caught." Braze cried.

"Okay so where's Red?" Skid asked looking down the "belly".

"They took her. Zadie wanted her because Messiah was paying her more attention and Pet was supposed to steal the stash for himself. So he could come up like Messiah. I'm so, so sorry."

"Oh you will be. Where are they?"

"I swear that's the only thing that I don't know. I swear." She said looking him in the face making sure he knew she was real.

Skid took out his Iphone frantically dialing Messiah's number to tell him everything that went down. He hoped he wouldn't be mad at him for leaving in the first place, blaming it all on him.

"What?" Messiah said trying to remain quiet as it was the middle of the night and nurses snapped about noise disturbing their patients. "Where's Red?"

"They got her, man."

"Damn." Messiah shook his head feeling like this shit was all his fault. "Alright, don't do anything, take Braze to the condos on Harlem and wait for my mark. I'm about…"

Messiah was halted when his other line rang. "Hold on."

He looked at the number and rolled his eyes answering it anyway. "Hello?"

"Yeah. I know I'm the last person you want to hear from right now but I need to talk to you bro." Danger said.

"I'm listening."

****

"Hey baby girl. Wake up." Zadie said.

Red grunted a little as she finally came to after two hours of unconsciousness. She looked around at her surroundings not knowing where the hell she was. Her head was banging really hard like she had been hit with a ton of bricks and her vision was a little blurry. She looked up and saw Pet sitting down in a chair and Zadie circling her like a piranha. Her hands were tied up above her head as she dangled from the ceiling as if she were a slaughtered cow. As her vision began to focus she realized that the breeze she was feeling wasn't a draft, she was completely naked.

"Bitch, what the fuck have you done to me?" Red asked sluggishly.

"I haven't done anything honey. Pet on the other hand…hm, he looks satisfied to me."

"You son of a bitch!" Red screamed.

Tears formed in her eyes but she refused to let them fall. She refused to let them see that she was hurt over the bullshit they had put her through. Her arms were beginning to feel sore from chains wrapped around her wrists pulling her upward. She felt her toes barely touching the ground swinging them desperately trying to wiggle her way to the ground.

"Oh now, no need for the pleasantries. I'm sure you can thank him later." Zadie laughed.

"Why are you doing this? What the fuck do you want?" Red
snarled.

"I want you to feel what I felt ever since you walked your bony
ass into the Shop. I was happy. I was about to marry this man
and then you came along and fucked his head up." Zadie slapped
her ass as she walked around her. "You fucked my money up."

"You stupid bitch. How could you marry an already married
man?"

Zadie picked up the long wooden paddle she had laying on the
floor and swung it around like it was a twirling baton. Red's
attitude was pissing her off to the fullest, wanting her to beg for
mercy instead of being bitchy and cocky.

"That man is mine. I don't know what the fuck you're talking
about but that man is mine and as soon as I get rid of you, we'll
be happy again."

"Are you fucking insane or just plain stupid? Messiah is married! He'll never love you, he'll never marry you. You were just
a hobby, a sport, something to do bitch when he got bored."

Zadie stopped twirling the paddle instantly letting the tip of
it hit the floor as her arm went limp. She could feel her boiling point being reached as her hand seemed to take on a mind of
it's own raising the paddle and knocking Red in the face with it.
Blood flew out of her mouth at the same time her face did while

Red coughed trying to collect herself. The blood tasted like copper in her mouth as she gathered enough of it in her mouth to spit out. She aimed for Pet but fell terribly short as he sat there with his legs crossed and a silly smile on his face like he was enjoying the show.

"Now bitch, you are going to suffer until your last heart beat. Maybe in your next life you'll learn not to fuck with bitches like me." Zadie whispered in her ear as she began beating her to a bloody pulp.

No nook or cranny would be left unturned on her body as she reached as far back as she could extending her arm as high as she could to deliver mighty blows to Red's backside, face, stomach and chest. She showed her no mercy becoming drunk from power with every stroke. She laughed horridly at the sound of Red's moans of pain.

Pet licked his lips and stroked his junk on the inside of his pants vigorously as he patiently awaited his turn with her glistening gloden body. He didn't care that blood would be dripping from almost every inch of her. All he could think of was the smell of her and her pussy on his flesh. Ever since she had walked into the Candy Shop he could think of nothing else but violating her, as he had done over and over again in his dreams. Even though her mouth would be saying no, in his mind all she was doing was begging for more.

Red tried to hold her sounds in but it was no use as she felt life slipping away from her with every blow. She lowered her head hoping to fall unconscious before the next blow and then ringing was heard in the distance. Zadie walked over to the crate that her phone was sitting on to view the number, angry that she had forgotten to put it on vibrate so she wouldn't be disturbed.

"Hello?" She answered letting the paddle drop to the floor seemingly out of breath.

"Yeah, um, we need to talk." Danger said.

"About what?"

"Yeah I don't think that's a good idea you know what I'm saying. I had a while to think about it, man. I could hook you back up with my brother. I know how to talk to him you know."

"Talk to him?"

Zadie was confused at what Danger was presenting to her but even more confused that Pet had gotten up and began sniffing Red's feet. He was sick, she knew, but to what extent she had no idea.

"Yeah, I mean you ain't gotta do all that revenge shit boo. You're too pretty for that you know. I gotchu just meet me at the Candy Shop in an hour. We can all sit in the office and talk." Danger said.

"The office?" Zadie bit her lip.

“Yeah, the office. What the fucks wrong with you kid? You acting crazy and shit man. The office, meet us at the office. You want this dude or not?” Danger became irate with her constant repeating.

“Naw, I'm good. I'm just wondering why you wanna help me. It just seems weird.”

“Well if you haven't heard, I'm fucking his wife. So when she gets out of her coma, that's my bitch you feel me. If you got him, he ain't gonna be thinking about her.”

“So it's true…he's married? Well…what about Red? I mean I'm sure he's into her so you don't need me.”

“Yeah he's married but he don't love her. Naw, Zadie, I just got off the phone with him and he ain't thinking about either one of their asses.”

Zadie's left eye flinched badly as she turned around looking at a bloody and bruised Red hanging from the ceiling as the light brightly lit the blood dripping from her body. Her mouth dropped open wondering what the fuck she had done. There was no way to undo the damage especially the shit at the Candy Shop so she wondered how she would get out of this one.

“Naw, um, why don't y'all meet me at my house. That way if everything goes right, you can leave us alone for the night.”

CC Alright bet." Danger hung up the phone.

He picked it back up dialing wildly.

CC Ayo, the shit is set."
****

Tina and Marie were showing the other seven soldiers how to capsulize the X. Pet wanted to get the shit out on the street as soon as possible since he was thirsty for money. He wanted to be Messiah so badly that he would be willing to kill his own mother to do it. He was ruthless like that and was tired of being a mere soldier to Messiah's every beck and call. The soldiers caught on right away thirsty to get money for themselves as well. All of them sampled as they packed giving them the proper rush they needed to complete the job.

CC Don't touch that shit. Pet is gonna snap if we fuck up his house. All we supposed to do is pack this shit." Tina said.

CC Well I'm tired of packing. That's all we ever do. They better pay us for all this shit yo." Marie replied.

CC Bitch, you're always complaining just get your ass over here and pack this shit before I slap your ass." Tina pointed to the floor next to her. "As soon as Pet becomes as large as Messiah is I'm hook that fool and the both of us will be home free. Okay baby?"

"I don't like the fact that you have to be the one to hook him. Why not me?"

"Cause my dear sweet Marie," Tina was kind then turned stern in under a minute, "you are weak and won't get him the way I will."

Marie was distraught at Tina's words but she leaned in and kissed her so fast that she didn't have time to react to it. Marie was a little touched in the head and Tina knew it, that's how she was able to take advantage of her and get her to do what she wanted. The soldiers were a bunch of horn dogs loving the show the ladies were putting on. They whistled and cheered them on telling them to take their clothes off.

"Get out!" Tina yelled. "Take this shit with you and finish downstairs."

Thought You Were Slick

Skid threw Braze in the car heading out to the condos just as Messiah had requested. He was beyond livid as he thought more and more how this was all her fault. She knew that shit would have never taken place with him there but he hated being involved in bullshit. The car was silent as they drove to the gate. Skid looked over at the first storage unit in the row and noticed that there was a flicker of light coming from underneath the open door. Those doors are always closed and locked tight so he didn't know what the fuck was going on in there but he figured some homeless dudes must've have breached the perimeter and had broken in.

"Don't fucking move or I'll blow your brains in right here, you got it?" Skid said pointing to Braze's forehead. She nodded her head profusely in agreement and watched as he got out of the car virtually tip toeing to the open storage unit. He secured his piece in his hand and raised the door aiming it and ready to shoot.

"What the fuck is going on in here?" Skid yelled looking confused at the scene his eyes were locked on.

What he saw would probably plague him for years to come. He thought he was imagining it but the more he blinked the more real it became. Bentley and his male friend were stretched out on the cold concrete floor crying hysterically while the two DEA agents were standing over them cheering and laughing. The agents looked at Skid grabbing their sides as if to snatch their guns out.

"Hold on! If y'all so much as blink, the last thing you'll see is black." Skid bellowed.

"Wait a minute now boy. Don't be a stupid here. We were just having a little fun here. You might wanna put that down cause it wouldn't be smart to shoot a couple of cops." Agent Maxwell said putting his hands up and patting the air as if to tell him to lower his weapon.

Agent Crosby took the cigarette out of his mouth and stood up waiting to see what Skid's next move was. He didn't care what anyone had to say; if Skid made the wrong move he would be pulling a cap out of his ass. Skid lowered his weapon but kept his finger posted on the trigger just in case any funny business kicked off. He watched as two skimpily dressed, worn down, piss invested, wrinkled up prostitutes continued to bounce up and down on the junks of Bentley and his lover. The smell eroding from in between their legs could stop someone's heart. Bentley and his friend cried like one-year-old babies wanting the whole ordeal to be over.

"Alright ladies. Let's call it a night." Maxwell said pulling out two hundred dollar bills from his pocket handing one to each of them as they pulled their tight glittering skirts back down. They walked out the door headed back to their little strip right on the bus stop across the street from the Shop.

"You son of a bitches!" Bentley barked grabbing his lover's hand to help him up. The men trotted across the way to Bentley's apartment above the office.

"I suggest you get out of here before he comes down with a shot gun ready to blow your fucking heads off." Skid said heading back to his car.

"Whoa. Not so fast. We came here looking for Messiah Torres and we ain't leaving 'til we get him." Maxwell replied.

"Well, I don't know where he is and good luck with that because I think I see Bentley loading up his shotgun through the window." Skid said getting in the car and hitting the button on the gate.

The agents saw that as their cue to leave having had enough fun for one night. Crosby tossed the cigarette into the storage unit as the two men dodged the closing gate headed back to the vehicle. They weren't concerned with Bentley or his retribution but they had bigger fish to fry and didn't want to stick around to make an already bad situation worst.

"You think he'll call the police?" Maxwell asked.

"That fag will have to prove it. It's our word, two decorated officers, against his."

****

Zadie rushed back to her house, leaving Pet behind with Red to keep an eye on her. She couldn't pass up an opportunity to get her man back especially since her main threat would be out of the picture. Something in her head clicked, thinking like she should feel a little bad for doing all of this to Red but she was still invading her territory. The bitch got what she deserved. She thought as she drove back to the house thinking of what dress she wanted to wear for her man. The thought of him already being married plagued her mind but she wasn't going to let that minor hurdle affect her feelings for him because in her mind she could easily be erased.

She made it to the house and raced to her bedroom picking out her black and white striped Nicole Miller jersey dress and laying it across the bed. She paired it with some white Jimmy Choo's and skirted off to the shower. She knew that this was the moment to look good for him and show him what he would otherwise be missing. She hit the shower scrubbing extra good making sure to hit every inch just in case he was feeling extra generous and wanted to give her kitty cat a lick. It would be a firstfor him since they've been messing around. Zadie grabbed a towel and dried off pinning her hair up in a nice tight bun leaving a few curly tendrils hanging down.

After she dressed, she but her makeup on extra thick and whorish just like he liked. Zadie left no stone unturned because tonight she was going to rock Messiah's world like she never did before. She went downstairs to her living room to check her cell to see if he or his brother had called her but there were no missed calls. She gazed out of the window to see if his car was out there but still nothing. A part of her began to worry wondering if Danger had kept his word to her. It would've broken her heart to know that he had lied to her.

"Pet is everything good." She asked.

"Yep, everything's wonderful over here." He said sounding out of breath.

"You haven't killed her yet have you? I don't know what I want to do yet."

"Naw, this bitch still breathing as far as I can tell. Shit at least her pussy is still warm." He said making slurping sounds.

"Ew. Fool you are nasty, yo. Oh well, do what you have to do but don't kill the bitch. I might have to use that hoe as bait. You need to chill for a minute and call them hoes at your house to make sure them dudes is packing that shit right." Zadie said dabbing Mac lip-gloss on her lips.

"I'm busy. Why can't you do it?"

"Because I don't want to be on the phone when he gets here now fucking call over there!" Zadie angrily hit the end button hanging up on him.

"I think it's a little too late for that don't you think?"

Zadie turned around startled to see Messiah sitting there in the darkness next to her fireplace. She hadn't anticipated him already being in her house and wondered how he even got in. He sat there leering out at her without a sound and never moving an inch. It was if he was studying her like a lab rat, watching her every move and storing it for further research. He sat with his legs crossed manly like and his fingers folded resting their tips on his upper lip.

"Hey baby. Uh, how long have you been sitting there?" She said attempting to pull her foot out of her mouth.

"Long enough to know that you are a lying, conniving little bitch." Messiah was surprisingly calm never bursting a blood vessel when he spoke.

"Baby, I..."

"Stop calling me that! I'm not now nor have I ever been your fucking baby. Bitch you're delusional. We had nothing. It was straight fucking. That's it."

"So that's all I was to you...pussy on a stick?"

"Basically. Now you're getting it. I never felt anything for you and I never will. Not to mention the fact that I'm married and had no intentions on leaving my wife. She's everything to me and you...you were something to do."

There were those words again. Zadie wasn't fond of being called "something to do". She couldn't stand the thought of someone one-upping her on a game she claimed to play so well. In her mind, she was beyond the shit and everyone needed to bow down to her every word. Rejection was not something Zadie was accustomed to or handle well. She was persistent like a motherfucka when it came down to shit she wanted and needed. It was get rich or die trying.

"Well, since I was just something to do how's about doing me right now for old times sake?" Zadie walked over to him pressing her body against him how he used to like.

Messiah strongly resisted her advances pushing her away so hard that shit landed on her ass. "Don't fucking touch me. I know everything. You thought you were slick but I know everything."

Zadie sat there pissed that he put his hands on her. The last man that did that ended up swimming with the fish in Lake Michigan, her father.

"Now where is she?"

"I don't know who you're talking about."

Umpf. Messiah delivered a punch dead in her mouth making her face hit the floor so hard it bounce back up. "Where is she?"

Zadie laughed like a grim reaper who had just stolen a soul. It was so evil and diabolical in nature that he couldn't comprehend why his punch didn't affect her. Blood dripped from her open mouth as she taunted him wanting more.

Umpf. He hit her again. She lay on the floor grasping her face trying to continue laughing and crawl through her blood to get away.

"Where is she?" He screamed at the top of his lungs feeling a demon of his own take over him.

He pulled her up by the thin collar of her dress hearing it tear just a little as he brought her up to his face wanting to spit in it badly. He was tired of repeating himself and threw her over on the couch then grabbed a poker from the fireplace and put it to her throat. Messiah was done playing with her ass. She thought this was all a game as if the pussy she gave him was credit enough to ensure he saved her life. Truth was, Zadie meant absolutely nothing to him. He only started kicking it with her when Alxeis started going sour on him and he needed that soft sensual comfort.

"If you don't tell me where she is now I'm going to stab you in your throat."

"What does it matter? If I tell you or not, you're still going to have your way with me. Just do it already! Just fucking kill me now!" Zadie snickered egging him on. "Com' on, Big Meech!"

Messiah got on his phone and dialed his brother.

"Hey, go to Pet's house." He said breathing heavily.

"Aight. Ayo, you straight?"

"Yeah, I'm good. Just make sure you ain't seen. No mistakes." He said hanging up the phone then turning to Zadie. "You trying to turn me back into the old me. I was almost to the point where I could be straight legit but what do you do?"

He looked down at her as she snickered in her own blood realizing that she would never tell him and by the time he reached her she could very well be dead.

****

"I bet you thought you were so pretty. Well you used to be, I'd give you that. But Z. fucked your ass up good, huh?"

Pet leaned in grabbing one of Red's tits and sucked on it roughly. "Do you like that? You know I used to fantasize about having sex with my little sister. You remind me of her in so many ways. You both have the same perky tits with the big brown nipples and you both have virtually hairless pussies. But I bet you shave yours, huh?"

He circled her, running his hand across her body then taking a bite on her ass letting the saliva drip from his mouth as he came up. Red was in and out of consciousness begging for death.

This fool had raped her so many times at this point she couldn't even keep count. As she prayed for her own death she prayed for his too. Every time he touched her she made sure to hold her pain inside. There was no way she was going to let this fool have the satisfaction of her tears. He walked around facing her front again and stared down at her vaginal slit.

"You must want me to touch you again. Is that it? You won't moan for me. Are you dead?" He asked sniffing her face. "Naw, you ain't dead."

He leaned in closer to sniff her scent some more and as he did Red snapped her mouth at him like a wild crocodile. She aimed for his ear but he leaned back swiftly and she missed by a hair.

"Oh, you almost got me there." He laughed. "You know my little sister was fourteen years old when I finally got that pussy. It's probably why my mother kicked me out but I got her good though. I got her drunk and made her think I was her boyfriend then I ate her pussy 'til she exploded." Pet grabbed the chair and walked it over sitting it in front of Red's legs. "You should've heard her moan. She was so loud that when my mother walked in I couldn't stop. I just needed to hear her scream some more. Is that what you want? Do you want me to lick that pretty pearl shit?"

Red kicked her legs trying to keep him from getting in between her legs. She didn't want his nasty corroded saliva on her pussy. He strong-armed her grabbing her thighs so they'd have little strength to move the he spread them eagle. He marveled in her opening beauty loving the way it looked and smelled even after hours of torture and rape. He stuck two fingers in her asshole pushing inside of her hard. She grunted and squirmed hoping to get him out of her but it was no use. He had a grip locked on her tighter spandex on belly fat. Pet planted his face in her middle slurping and munching like he was at the last supper.

Red felt nauseous as chunks rose in her throat closing in on her mouth. She opened her mouth letting the vomit ooze out and down her navel to the top of Pet's head. He pretended not to care and kept going like nothing had changed. Red continued to dry heave vomit as she urinated a little in his mouth with every squeeze. Pet never budged a muscle. To him he was eating the ultimate feast.

Inferno

Tina pulled Marie's shirt off lifting it above her head as she kneeled down to kiss on the plumped cleavage staring back at her. She threw the shirt on the floor as Marie stroked her short bobbed hair loving the feeling that pulsated through her body right down to her clitoris. She wanted her so badly but didn't know what she was doing as this would be her first time with a female. Marie had always fantasized what it would be like to grab a woman's breasts and suck on her warm supple nipples. She had always wanted to know what it felt like to have a woman's sexy sultry body pressed against hers. Marie was a romantic who thought her first time with a female would be magical with rose petals and scented candles everywhere, not in the middle of a potential trap house.

She raised her ass up to unbutton and remove her jeans from her backside kicking them off with her feet then spreading eagle revealing a pink slightly hairy opening. Tina moaned enticingly as she moved in for the kill. Marie rubbed her nipples continuously aching for a piece of Tina's tongue as she teased her flicking her tongue back and forth on her clitoris slightly just enough to get it tingling.

"Oh my GOSH! Just fucking do it already!" Marie screamed pushing her face into her awaiting pussy.

Tina's face was embedded into her lovely goodness devouring every single drop that Marie set free. As Marie moaned uncontrollably, Tina mocked her sounds moaning and humming on her snatch making a vibrating motion and sending chills through her body. Tina slid her finger in and out of her pussy continuously splashing in her warm goodness and ramming inside of her hard.

"Lemme do you." Marie screamed unaware of the snickering happening on the other side of the door.

The soldiers were listening in getting erections and stroking their egos as they listened wanting to burst in on them and get a piece of the action. Tina raised her head hearing the commotion but paid it no mind. She didn't care if they listened so long as they couldn't see. She looked over at Marie's sex face and slid her head back in between her legs. Marie needed more than just having her pussy ate and pushed her head away scooting back on the bed.

"Come here, baby. Lemme do you." She requested.

"Naw you ain't ready for that yet." Tina said laying back on the bed.

"Don't tell me what I'm ready for. I'm a big girl. I can handle this."

Tina looked at her with a discerning expression on her face. "You sure about that?"

Marie crawled on top of Tina rolling her shirt up, kissing her cleavage like she was kissing her grandmother's cheek. She had no idea what she was doing and Tina's patience was wearing thin. She couldn't wait for her to discover the strength inside of her and get down to business.

"You need to get with it. You said you wanted to do this, so do it." Tina snarled.

"I am, dang. Why you gotta be so forceful?"

"Cause you're scary. Don't talk about it, be about it suga."

Marie snapped her bra off allowing her pretty red breasts to bounce out. The sights of her red nipples made her pussy throb as she grabbed them rubbing her face in them like a dog. She finally put them in her mouth and sucked on them moving back and forth between the two like she was a hungry baby looking for milk. Tina rubbed Marie's clit making her knees buckle as she sucked harder and squeezed harder on her breasts. Tina was not amused and felt nothing from it, rolling her eyes not wanting to waste anymore time. She unlatched Marie from her breasts pushing her head downward to her jeans. Marie got the hint and got a shot of confidence from out of nowhere.

"You want me to lick this pussy, bitch?" Marie asked unbuttoning and struggling to slide Tina's jeans of her ass.

CCI want you to do something more than what you were doing, I'll tell you that."

Marie laughed Tina's cockiness off finally ripping the jeans off and tossing them over her shoulder playfully throwing them on the floor. She tried to playful seduce Tina just as she had done her by breathing heavily over her canary yellow panties hoping to make her pussy pulsate. She went to remove her panties slowly inching them off looking her in the eye and smiling ready to devour her and prove to her she was much more than just a pretty face. She wanted to make Tina fall in love with her overnight simply by one night of tasting.

CCCut the light off." Tina requested.

CCNo, I wanna see this pretty pink pussy and lick every inch of it."

CCBitch just caught the light off."

Marie ignored her. She ripped the panties off her legs flinging them across the room playfully. Tina had closed her legs so tightly that Marie couldn't get in between. She laughed it off though trying to pry her legs open and get inside. Tina finally slowly opened her legs and leaned her head back on the headboard giving in to Marie's advances. Marie leaned in and spread her legs forcefully then placed her chin on top of her clit moving it around in a circular motion. Tina giggled knowing that this chick had no idea what she was doing. She lay there and waited for her to get it right but she was taking forever and Tina's pussy was becoming moist.

Marie realized that the minor seduction wasn't working as well as she had hoped so she went in for the kill planting her mouth right on her clit sucking like it was a lollipop. Tina moaned frenziedly squirming as her voice became high pitched and she clenched the pillow on the side of her. Marie sucked away with her eyes closed loving the bobbing motion she was making and the noise eroding from Tina. Then Marie slowed her motion gradually opening her eyes feeling that something was wrong. She bobbed her head to a slow stop then rose from up off of Tina. Tina's screams came to a screeching halt, as she grew more pissed by the minute.

"Why'd you stop?" Tina said slowing her breathing.

"Um, Tina. What the hell is that?"

"What?"

"Your clit…it's…it's huge!"

"Oh that. That's nothing, Marie. Keep going." Tina exclaimed pushing her back unto the enormous clitoris.

"No. NO! There's something wrong with your fucking clitoris. It looks like…like a dick."

"What? Tramp, you're crazy. Eh. Now are you going to finish or not?"

"Hell naw, I'm not going to finish. You need to get that thing tested or something." Marie hopped off the bed putting her clothes back on laughing at Tina's deformity. "I mean you could fuck me with that thing if you wanted to. Damn and it grew in my mouth."

Marie kept on talking about it as the women located their clothes. Tina slammed around things feeling uncomfortable talking about it. She knew what it was and why it was there but she chose not to disclose that information to Marie. She didn't feel like she owed anyone an explanation for anything.

"Hey, why don't you just shut the fuck up, huh?" Tina said pulling her shirt on over her head.

"Okay, okay. But I'm just saying you could get paid with that thing ya know? Some men like big clits. Shit maybe Pet will love it. But I'm not putting that shit back in my mouth."

"Shut the fuck up!"

"All I'm saying is maybe you should think about getting a clit reduction. It might be healthier for you or your relationships."

"Shut UP!"

"You know what it's like? It's like you have the best of both worlds. You're a man and a female. You could fuck and get fucked all in one sitting."

Marie rambled on and on about it like it was the weirdest thing she'd ever had in her mouth at one time. Sweat began to form on Tina's forehead as she tried to put her words out of her mind but she just wouldn't leave it alone. Tina walked towards the door needing some space from her until she could clear her head about the first reaction she's ever experienced with her condition. She felt messed up in the head because she usually never let anyone down there and didn't know why today was such an exception. She felt helpless and out of control and that feeling killed her inside.

"Hey, when you go out there, can you send one of those real mean in here. Now my pussy's wet and I need a nice long dick to bang me. Yours is too little." Marie laughed.

She was having a field day taunting Tina since she had her ass on her shoulders twenty-four hours a day. It was about time she got a taste of her own medicine. Tina turned around staring at Marie confused at how the tables had turned. She boiled with madness and became intoxicated with rage. Tina roared like a lioness as she lunged at Marie grabbing her head and slamming it into the floor.

"What the hell is wrong with you? Get off me! Get off me!" Marie yelled as Tina climbed on top of her scratching for her neck.

Marie punched at Tina's face like a punching bag but it was as if Tina couldn't feel a thing. Her eyes were opened wide and didn't blink not even for a second. She finally had at Marie's neck and squeezed beyond measure. Her fingers acted like a Boa Constrictor squeezing and engulfing until it's prey could take no more. Tina began smiling and madly wanting more, hoping for sudden death. Marie gasped for air begging her for her life. She didn't know that one night of pleasure would end costing her a world of pain. She scratched, tugged, kicked, and pulled at Tina but nothing would relinquish her grip from her neck. Tina shook her head faster and squeezed tighter and tighter until Marie's body had given up and completely gone limp.

****

Danger and Amy crept through the backyard of Pet's house dressed in dark colored clothing with two big black back-packs strapped to their backs. They were as quiet as church mice scaling the back of the bungalow house like highly trained ninjas in the night. Amy was the brain behind Danger's brawn as she ran up the back porch stairs peeking in the back windows trying to see the inhibitor's locations.

"Hey babe, check out that lumber over there. You thinking what I'm thinking?"

"Hell yeah. Let's do this." Danger said amped up. "But are you and my seed okay for this?"

"Will you stop worrying about us? I live for this shit and with any luck this baby is gonna be as ruthless as his momma so you need to quit trippin." Amy said walking up grabbing his ears gently stroking them as she spoke.

"Okay since I'm already back here, I'll do the back and since you look like a tall grim reaper at night with that black on, you do the front." Amy said kissing his lips seductively before she grabbed a few two-by-fours and headed for the back door.

Danger wanted to resent that statement but he knew they had no time for the semantics. He ran around to the front of the house with two long two by fours of lumber then place then up against the wooden door's knob and kicking them at the bottom to ensure it was secured tightly. He could hear Amy setting up the same action in the back. The soldiers heard the noises plain as day and ran to the doors and windows looking out to see what was going on. Danger stood looking at them with a devilish smile on his face. He fed off of their fear loving each and every moment of the last breaths they relished. He reached in his open backpack and pulled out two glass Molotov cocktail bombs and lit them never taking his eyes off of them. The men raised their guns aiming to fire as Danger threw the bombs simultaneously into the door's window and the living room window.

When she heard the glass breaking in the front, Amy threw her bombs through the back windows as well. She saw one of the soldiers trying to escape via the window and lit another one throwing it in his face. The man screamed in agony as he retreated back inside the house. The house lit up like a burning inferno as the man caught on fire pumped around into various things before falling to the floor out of her sight. She looked around making sure no one else was trying to escape when she found a fool had crept out of one of the side windows and was headed right for her.

A my quickly removed her 9mm pistol silencer from behind her back and drove two right in his ass. She embedded one in his stomach and another in his forehead swiftly. He dropped like a bad habit to the grass. She kneeled down pointing the gun checking her surroundings with a keen eye almost like a ninja then looked up at the roof detecting movement. There was someone up there crouching down trying hard as hell not to be seen. She looked trying to make out who it was but it was no use, the darkness and the smoke eroding from the house took over. She figured as long as they weren't planning to attack her they were good with her for the moment and ran around to the front of the house to meet Danger.

D anger grabbed her and stood there holding her as if they were in front of some romantic candle light dinner. The retched sounds of death and the smell of burnt flesh began to fill the air. Amy tapped Danger's butt giving the signal that it was time to go as the couple ran back around the house through the yard into their getaway car. They slapped hands for a job well done and smiled at each other feeling like they were the shit. Danger got on his phone and made the call.

"It's all good over here."

Pray For Sweet Death

"Did you get any info?"

"Huh, naw man. They was all on dummy." Danger said side eyeing Amy.

"Damn it!"

Messiah hung up the phone and sat on the couch rubbing his head in total dismay at how long this chick was holding out. She was truly a soldier taking her beating and still ticking. He needed to crack her in a way that would make her submit once and for all.

"Don't you have a son at your grandmother's house that you don't take care of?"

"What?" Zadie was at full attention staring up at Messiah from the floor.

"Struck a nerve, huh?"

She sat in silence with her head down. Her son had never been brought up before since she gave up her rights to her grandmother five years ago. When she went over to visit him he knew her as Aunt Z. Now he was ten years old and had found out the truth from other relatives talking about it in his face. She would go over and he would treat her like a bum on the street, straight trash. It killed her inside but she had no other choice but to give him up or he would've ended up just like her, a big fat failure. She kicked her shoes off and stood barefoot toe to toe with Messiah.

"If you want to be a low down dirty bastard and involve my son then go right ahead. But know this only snakes fuck with kids." Zadie said.

"Bitch you think you gonna guilt me into some shit? That girl you got somewhere fucked up is a damn kid herself. You wasn't thinking about her life so why the fuck should I care about your son's?"

"What you jealous cause your crack head ass wife can't have any kids?"

"How the fuck did you find that out?"

"What are you talking about?"

"Who told you?" Messiah became furious and slapped her back down to the floor.

He didn't realize that she was just blowing smoke and couldn't have possibly known about it. But her words were enough to fuel the fire within him. He picked up the phone and dialed furiously.

"You on your way? Bet." Messiah hung up the phone as quickly as he picked it up.

Zadie knew he had just ordered the hit on her son but she couldn't bring herself to say anything. It was like saving face was more important than saving her innocent son's life. A lump rose in her throat and tears sparked from her eyes as she sat on the floor licking the blood from her lip. As a single tear wept from her eye and hit the floor in the middle of a small pool of blood, she watched as it spread and mixed in with her plasma creating a shape she thought to be a heart. It was her sign that regardless of what happened to her she could not bring herself to let her seed get mixed up in her bullshit.

****

"Hey babe. I think I know where Red is. We're literally right around the corner from the joint." Danger said to Amy as he let his foot sleep on the gas trying to hurry to the location.

He remembered the conversation he had with Zadie in the car by the lake and knew that's exactly where she was.

"How do you know where she is?"

"I remember them talking about it." Danger lied.

"Mmhmm." Amy folded her arms and sat back in her seat staring out the window seemingly annoyed.

D anger turned the music up hoping to diffuse the interrogation and get back to the matter at hand, finding Red. He drove on through stop signs and sometimes through red lights trying to get there before it was too late. He turned the corner cutting his lights off when he hit 119th Street and road down to the end of the block to the old Frito Lay factory. It had been abandoned for almost five years due to the economy and was now only frequented by crack heads, homeless people, and old alchies.

"Babe you stay here in the car. This could get ugly and I'm not putting my baby in harm's way."

A my looked at Danger crooked eyed and smacked her lips. "Are you serious?"

"Naw, I'm just bullshitting. But stay behind me ya heard?"

S he nodded her head like whatever as they exited the car and walked around to the side of the building with the most light shining. They crept up to look through the windows but couldn't get a good view since they were both too short to reach them even with Danger being almost six feet tall. Danger signaled to Amy in informal sign language that he was going to give her a boost to see if she could see anything. She signaled that he better not drop her. He looked at her like she had to be kidding. Danger locked his hands tight and positioned them as he formed a squatting stance. Amy grabbed hold of his shoulders and mounted up as Danger boosted her up toward the window. She held for a few seconds then dropped down.

"Well?" He whispered.

"There is a man and a woman in there. Whether it's them or not, I don't know." She whispered back.

Danger shook his head. He figured if it was a loving couple then he would apologize for disturbing them but if it was some dickhead in there with Red, then he would kick his monkey ass. He prepared Amy and signaled for her to stay directly behind him at all cost, yet again. Amy waved him forward as the two turned grabbing their 9mm pistol silencers from behind their backs and prepared to ambush the people inside.

"Hold it motherfucka! Moving would be a mistake. My girl here is deadly with this weapon. She'll drive one in you before you get a chance to exhale, dog." Danger said disgusted by the scene before him.

Pet slowly eased his piece out of Red's now sore and torn backside. She let out a sigh of relief knowing that the torture and sodomy was over but she still prayed for the sweet victory of death. She didn't see any reason for her existence to keep being treated like waste in a garbage disposal. Amy followed behind Danger as he moved in gradually towards Red trying to see if she was still alive as she just hung there dangling without so much as moving a fingertip.

"Go see if she's okay baby, I got you." Danger told Amy as she moved over toward Red never taking her eyes off of Pet. "Pet, you need your ass whooped, man."

"How the fuck you gonna judge me, D? You slip your dick in anything that breaths on you wrong and you got the nerve to judge me."

Amy side eyed Danger but knew this wasn't the time or the place to bring the shit up. She had her pistol in one hand as she backed up to the wall tracing the chains that were bound to Red. At the wall, she found the chain rolled up around an old pipe and began to release it, watching as Red was lowered to the ground.

"Chump, I ain't rapin' females though you nasty motherfucka."

"Yeah, well, everybody has their own shit going on. This shit is mine. Shit, if you didn't keep her so cuffed up, I would've raped yo bitch."

JUPE!

Before she realized it, Amy had shot one time into Pet's arm. "Oops, my bad."

"AH! You bitch! You shot me!" Pet exclaimed pissed that Zadie had left him there without a pistol to defend himself. He couldn't wait to get back to the crib to get his piece he swore revenge on both of them. "Man, D, why don't you let me go this one time dude. I promise I'll leave town and you will never have to see me again, man. Just give me one chance to make it right."

"Not my call." Danger said as he kept aim on him like a hawk on a rabbit and took out his phone to call Messiah. "Yo man. We got her."

"Straight?"

"So far."

"Good looking." Messiah said exhaling in relief.

"One."

As soon as Danger hung up his phone, Pet made a break for it pushing his arms up in the air hoping to make him drop his gun. Danger was solid though and began blasting at him along with Amy. Pet was hit again in the shoulder but was like a track star having ran so fast that he got out the door anyway.

"Stay here." Danger said as he ran out the door like a detective trying to catch the fugitive.

"Girl, are you okay?" Amy said detaching the chains from around Red's flimsy wrist.

She sat her up covering her body with a dirty dingy towel that was lying on the floor. The factory floor was cold and icky but it was relief to Red not having her body stretched beyond belief anymore. She trembled not muttering a word just wanting to go home and get in a shower never to get out.

"That son of a bitch is gone. I couldn't catch his ass." Danger came back in out of breath.

"We need to get her to a doctor." Amy suggested helping her to her feet but she fell back down instantly, so weak from the nightmare.

"No." She said in a raspy voice. "No doctor."

"Girl you might have some shit you can't get rid of. Now let's gone ahead to the emergency room. You ain't gotta tell 'em shit if you don't want to but you gotta go." Danger said sternly.

Red wasn't in any mood or condition to argue with anyone so she just followed them out the door. She really didn't care at this point she was just happy to be around people who weren't going to hurt her, she hoped.

****

"Messiah, please call off your goons. Don't hurt my son. I'll tell you...I'll tell you." Zadie said crawling on her hands and knees reaching and tugging on Messiah's pants.

He kicked her off of him figuring she had found her heart right there. But what she didn't know was that Danger had already called him with the news that Red was safe and sound. Unbeknownst to her, her plan had failed miserably and as he looked onto her bloody and bruised face he felt no sympathy for her or her cronies.

"Naw Z, you need to suffer just like Red suffered. Maybe next time you will have the same kind of mercy on your next victim that you're asking me for."

The darkness was gradually turning into light as the daybreak was upon them. Zadie began balling seeming virtually inconsolable hoping that she would be able to see her son one last time to tell him she was sorry for involving him in all of this. She wanted one more chance to be a real parent to him, to perhaps take him to a basketball game or just give him a hug and tell him she loved him. His youth had only just begun and it seemed because of her ruthless selfish ways it would be stripped away for eternity.

"Shut the hell up. Alright, I'll give you one chance to redeem yourself. Tell me everything that happened tonight and if you don't, well, take a look outside." Messiah pointed to the car sitting in front of the house with the motor running.

Zadie got up and walked to the window to look out at the car. She could only see a person sitting in the passenger seat with a black linen bag over their head. There was no way to make out who was actually sitting there but knowing Messiah and what he was capable of she didn't want to take her chances. She sat down on the couch with her hand raised to her mouth in shock at the turn of events that had taken place this whole night.

"Okay, we did it. We did it all." Zadie confessed.

"Did what with who?" Messiah asked fiddling with his phone.

"I set the plan in motion for Pet, Tina, and Marie to ransack the joint and kidnap Red. They stole about a million dollars worth of merch and then Pet brought Red to the warehouse on 119th." Zadie paused wondering if she should say anymore. "I didn't mean for anybody to get hurt."

"What about Braze?"

"Braze was the guinea pig. We just told her to do something and she did it no questions asked. All you gotta do is throw some money at her and she's down."

"That's one hell of a way to talk about your sister."

"She's a hoe. She gets down. That's just how she is, I don't have to sugar coat it. I love her but it is what it is."

"Really?" Messiah said giving a backwards look.

It pained Messiah to know that Braze was in on the whole operation with those idiots. He had a soft spot in his heart for her because she was carrying a son. His son. It was a secret she hid very well from everyone and he appreciated that about her. But she knew something was going down regardless of if she knew exactly what was going to happen or not. He was hurt by her blatant disregard to say something and her need to do anything for a quick buck. There was no emotion displayed on his face, as he turned toward the fireplace so disgusted at the sight of Zadie.

"Okay so why did you do it?" Messiah asked staring up at the ceiling trying to regroup his thoughts.

"Because...you had stopped showing me the affection you once showed me before Red came here." She paused. "I didn't care anything about the money or the merch, I just wanted you back."

Messiah dropped his head realizing that ways and thinking brought about a sudden chain of events that could have readily been avoided. But she was selfish and stupid and only thinking of herself and her greed. He turned around looking down upon her weeping eyes. Her mascara had run all down her cheeks and her tears flowed continuously. She hoped he would feel some kind of sympathy for her and have mercy enough to take her back and forget all about everything that took place but she knew that would be a shot in hell.

Don't Be A Fool

Skid looked over at Braze feeling sorry for her. He didn't know what Messiah had in store for her but he knew whatever it was he sure didn't want to be in her shoes. Even though he liked her there was nothing he could do. She had played a big girl's game and now she must suffer the consequences. He rolled the window all the way down and lit his cigarette on the outside of the car. He took a couple of pulls before hearing the faint sounds of tears under the black satin bag over Braze's head.

"What you crying for?" He asked solemnly.

"I'm scared. Why do I have to wear this thing over my head with my hands up?" Braze asked trembling.

"Because you can't know where you are right now." Skid replied.

"But why? I didn't do anything wrong. I can't believe this bitch got me mixed up with this shit."

"Well, you're a little big girl. You're responsible for your own destiny. Can't nobody control that but you."

Braze lowered her head in shame. She couldn't believe that he could do that to her baby's daddy. A man she had no intentions on being with but seeing him with her sister drove her insane. Zadie always rubbed Messiah in Braze's face and couldn't wait to talk to her about their sex-capades. But Braze never came at her about the issue since she had something he would never give Zadie, his seed. She would often dream about one day becoming his wife and having three or four more kids for him but she felt that she would never fully have him or his heart. She didn't fully trust a man who worked around half naked women all night, but the few magical nights they shared together trying to make their baby were the best nights of her life. Messiah was never a man to just fuck you and forget you. He was always gentle, he was always loving, and he was always sensual when it came down to it.

"I just want him to know that I know I fucked up and I'm sorry." Braze said waiting for a response from Skid.

Skid knew better than to get too attached to these females. If he did he wouldn't be able to function always dealing with their tears and emotions.

"What do you think he's going to do to me?" Braze asked quietly looking in his direction.

"I don't know. He told us to drive out here for something but whatever it is…I guess we'll know soon enough."

****

" Ma'am, I need to know what happened to you or else we can't help you." The officer said writing things down on her notepad.

" I can't. I won't."

" If he got away, think of all the other women out there he might be doing this to. Think of the ones who are just like you and are scared to say anything. Don't live in fear, Redina. Take back your life."

The words that the female cop said to Red resonated with her as she looked up at her with the only eye that wasn't swollen shut. If she let this beat her than everything she would have gone through would be in vain. She had been through so much and even sold herself to eat. She had seen her family brutally murdered for the love of money and gluttony. She had single handedly achieved her revenge against the man who murdered her parents, Elias Gonzalez, so why was it trivial for her to report Pet to the police? She gave the nice policewomen the information they needed to hunt and locate Pet but she knew they would never find him. He was like Big Foot, oddly elusive. But knowing he was still out there only meant one thing for Redina Hawkins, revenge would be sweeter than life itself.
****

Messiah grew weary of the song and dance happening in Zadie's living room and was ready to put an end to it once and for all. He took out his cell once more and dialed eagerly on the keypad. Zadie was leaning forward on the couch with her fingers locked and elbows to her knees, shaking her head. She didn't know what Messiah had in store for her but she felt that whatever it was, after everything she had done, she down right deserved it.

CCYeah, meet at the spot." He said hanging up the phone and grabbing Zadie by the arm tightly.

The small array of sunlight slapped her face as she squinted and shielded her eyes. He led her around the back to the alley and threw her into the passenger seat of a van. As he got in and started the car he looked at her with beady eyes snickering just a bit. He was a bit excited to get to his destination driving like a bat out of hell. What Zadie didn't realize is that right behind them in a dark vehicle was Skid and her sister driving to same location. She looked around trying to make sure they weren't going to any open fields or ditches because if they were she had already made plans to jump out and run for her life. If she was going to go down she was damn well going to go down swinging.

Zadie recognized the route they were taking and knew it well. She leaned back in the seat feeling comfortable and relieved feeling like there she had nothing to worry about. Messiah would never bring bullshit to his establishment because that was his legitimate business and no one knew of its underground layer. He always kept it professional and never brought dirt in. They pulled up to the gate flowing through with ease as the gate slid over allowing both cars to slip in.

The sunlight slammed smack dab in their faces now as they drove into the horizon down the long neighborhood of storage units. Zadie sat up noticing Danger's car already parked outside then turning around noticing another car behind them pulling up. She was still confident in her safety but wondered how long that would last.

They jumped out the car, Messiah signaling for her to come by his side as Skid and the masked and tied hostage walked up to them. The storage unit gate went up as they walked in not waiting for it to fully rise then walked into the awaiting elevator. Zadie stared at the masked hostage already knowing who it was. She knew who it was since it was hard not to notice a protruding belly despite the mask. She knew they had weaseled some information out of her seeing as though she was just that weak. Zadie wanted to reach up and hit her in the stomach just for being a dumb ass all the time but knew this wasn't the time nor the place. It was then that she realized that her son was never in that car. The whole time it was Braze with the bag over her head and Messiah had played her yet again.

On the bottom floor, Messiah walked through the hideous display that used to be the business he had worked so hard to create. He kicked the left over bags out the way making his way down the "belly" looking at the empty brightly lit rooms. Years of hard worked gone to shit in an instant. He thought. Danger and Amy stepped out the room with their arms folded hawking as they all walked up to them. Skid removed the bag and the zip tie from Braze's head and hands. She looked around at everyone and felt her heart drop when she saw Zadie standing no less than a few steps from her. She wasn't scared of her but she definitely didn't feel comfortable standing so close to her. Zadie, on the other hand, didn't even bat at a lash her.

CC Now that we're all here, we can finally air out all grievances and when we leave here today, there will be no hard feelings in the Candy Shop." Messiah said as watched the dogs roam around freely around them.

S kid stepped back leaning against the wall already having a feeling of what was going down. He knew Messiah wasn't the type to really hit a female but it was clear that there were a few ass beatings a bit overdue. Messiah walked around Braze licking his lips and giving her the short look at the same time. He but his love for her aside to handle business. He was at witts end with all the females in his life but he remembered she was the only one carrying his seed.

CC Braze. What can I say to you? You disappointed me but more importantly you broke my heart." Messiah said cracking his knuckles. "Zadie. Willing to sell your soul for a quick buck and some change. What do I do with the both of you?"

T he ladies lowered their heads in shame then Zadie picked hers back up in anger.

CC It wasn't all me, Meech. There was Pet and the rest of the soldiers and, and…"

CC And who?"

CC Your own fucking brother, Danger."

The room grew cold and everybody stood still as all eyes turned to the elephant in the room.

"You dirty little bitch! How the hell you gonna put me in that shit with you, Z?"

"Oh don't act so innocent you fucking spaz! You met up with me in the car that day we was smoking weed and you were all game for it." Zadie said pointing and snarling at him. "Meech he was only out to replace you and get the money out of your safe. He's just as much at fault as we are."

"Uh, huh. So how do you think I found out about this whole thing going down? Magic?" Messiah said scratching his eyebrow.

Zadie paused then turned back to Danger giving him the evil eye. It was he who foiled her plan and set her up from the get-go. If it weren't for her naïve love of Messiah she wouldn't have fallen for that phone call Danger hit her with and she would've gotten away with the whole thing. She thought about the plan wishing she had done a few things differently to have been on top of her game.

"If you weren't such a conniving bitch maybe none of us would be in this mess." Braze said looking down to the floor.

"What did you just say?" Zadie asked walking up to her sister's ear. "Did you have something to say to me?"

"Yeah. You fucked up a good thing. We were getting money, real money, and we didn't have to flip burgers or sell our asses to get it but you jacked that up for everybody." Braze snapped back at her.

CCYou stupid cunt! If it weren't for me you wouldn't even have been here.
You would have been still stuck at home up under Grammy, watching my son, and eating Donut Sticks all damn day."

B raze became furious at the way Zadie was talking to her. She talked as if she was nine years old all over again. She hated that Zadie never respected her as a woman and always belittled her.

CCYou know that's mighty funny. You're absolutely correct. If it weren't for you I wouldn't have known about the Candy Shop since you whored around to get in here and I wouldn't have met Big Meech and gotten pregnant with his son..." Braze paused with a smile on her face. She looked up into Messiah's eyes waiting to see if he would trip that the cat was out of the bag but he didn't. "Oops! Did I just say that? Yep, I think I did."

Z adie lost it grabbing Braze's hair throwing her to the floor. She climbed on top of her hoping to bash her giant head into the concrete but was immediately pulled away by Skid who manhandled her like a rag doll.

CCGet your ass back over there. " He said. "Ain't none of that going down."

Z adie retreated back against the wall she was thrown up against breathing heavily. She looked into Messiah's cold pitiless eyes hoping for an ounce of it. He looked away not wanting to let her make an ass out of herself any further by assuming he did. She looked around at the faces glaring and the eyes haunting her. They never had any intention on forgiving this deed she had done but she wasn't about to let them think they had the upper hand on her. Hell naw, she wasn't going out like a punk.

"You people are weak. You wish you had the balls I had to do this shit.
I see what I want and I go get it. I wanted Meech and I got him. I wanted to be the top bitch and I was. You motherfuckas were like putty in my hand. Don't you see?" She recited drunk with rage and what she thought was power.

"You're so fucked up in the head you don't realize you're losing." Messiah said.

"We could've been happy you and me."

"Yeah and now it's over."

BANG! BANG! BANG! BANG!

Red stepped out of the office pointing a long black 9mm gun inserting two slugs into Zadie's head and two in her chest. Zadie slid down the wall leaving small a blood streak with her eyes still focused in on her one true love. A loud screeching shriek thundered out of Braze's mouth. She crawled over to her sister's lifeless body pulling and grabbing on her rocking her gently. She put her head under her chin and stroked her hair pretending she was only sleeping and would wake up soon then let out another high pitched shriek. Messiah pointed at her for Skid to pick her up and carry her into the meeting room away from the dead body. He looked up at a badly beaten and bruised Red and walked over to touch her face. She lowered her gun jumping a little still on edge from the whole ordeal she had just been through.

"You satisfied?" He asked stroking her hair.

"No. I won't be satisfied until they're all dead. Including you princess." Red said pointing over into the room at a terribly distraught Braze.

"I didn't do anything, Red. I didn't know what they would do to you."

Red shook her head not giving a shit what she had to say. "Pray I have mercy on you because you're Messiah's baby's momma. But know this, that ass is on the line."

Her words only made Braze more hysterical.

"We will talk Red."

"We've done enough talking don't you think?"

Messiah was surprised at the sudden change in tone from her. He figured she would be happy to see him, when in fact she wasn't happy at all. It was as if her spirit was ripped from her when they kidnapped her and committed all of those unspeakable acts on her. He knew he would have to bring her back to life. He wouldn't let her destroy herself because of that shit.

❝You know I had you the whole time, right? I wasn't going to give up until I got you back." Messiah said.

❝I know." Red replied.

Messiah's cell rang and vibrated out of control the whole time and continued to do so. He finally picked it up checking out the caller ID and saw that the doctor from the hospital had been calling his ass off. He wanted to check the billionth voicemail that he had left but noticed Red heading for the elevator as she stepped over Zadie's lifeless body like she was scraps of trash.

❝You guys think you can clean this mess up and take out the trash." He said pointing to Zadie's empty shell.

❝We got you bro. Don't worry about this." Danger replied.

He took the pistol from Red handing it to Amy then grabbed Red's hand escorting her to the elevator with him. She was confused as to where he was taking her but didn't ask any questions looking down at the ground not wanting him to stare at her swollen face and badly beaten eye. She was vexed at the fact that all of this happened to her over a love she hadn't actually owned. She was beginning to think that accepting Messiah's help was the biggest mistake of her life. Even the streets hadn't prepared her for the things she's been through all while working at the Candy Shop. A candy that was more bitter than sweet.

"I want you to go to the hospital with me to check on my wife." He said as they stepped out the elevator.

"What? Are you crazy? I'm not going to the hospital with you."

"Why not? She's in a coma so she won't even know you're there."

"Messiah, has this night got you fucked up or something? No, I'm not doing it."

"Red, you're overreacting…"

"No! You're losing your damn mind. Look, let's just call this what it is. I work for you, nothing more nothing less. I've been through enough in my life I don't need to add a man and his drama to the equation."

Messiah rubbed his head in confusion. The only other woman to reject him was his wife, which was probably the reason why he was so drawn to her. Red tried to walk off but remembered that she didn't have the app for the door so she stood there in silence waiting for him to raise the door. She turned her back to him with her arms folded knowing how much it burned her inside to ignore him. But she wasn't about to come second to nobody, not even for him.

"Red…"

"Good-bye Messiah."

Messiah wasn't about to let her go that easy. He wanted to remain true to his wife but there was no way in hell he was prepared to lose the only thing that was pure and made him happy. She could be mad all he wanted at him but he wanted her affection, he yearned for it. In the back of his mind he knew it was right but the only way he was going to remain sane with Alexis was by having Red right there by his side. hit the keypad opening the unit door and they stepped out as the sun shone down hard on their faces.

"You thought I was playing motherfucka?" Bentley said raising the Sawed-off shotgun up to Agent Crosby's face.

"Alright now. You don't want to do anything stupid. Killing a DEA agent is a federal offense son. You want to end your life right here?" Crosby said damn near about to shit on himself.

"Crosby, what are you doing here?" Messiah asked.

"He's been here all night, Meech, snooping around and shit. He's been spying on your operation. Why can't black folk just have a legitimate business without being harassed, huh?" Bentley snapped becoming jittery.

He was waving the gun around and pointing it up and down from Crosby's schlong back up to his face trying to decide on which one he wanted to blast him in first. Bentley had five o'clock shadow like he hadn't shaved or slept in days but the incident happened only a matter of hours before. He looked as if he had been up all night cracked out on a heroin binge, a substance abuse he knew all too well. Messiah got him clean and kept him that way for 5 years and he reverted back to the same shit after a matter of hours. Messiah knew exactly what it was because he could never forget the ghost-like image that always appeared on his face. It was like he was dead already.

" What the fuck are you doing, B?" Messiah yelled. "Man put the damn gun down!"

" Bentley!" Red shouted.

Bentley raised the gun even higher aiming directly for the spot in between Crosby's eyes. He wanted that son of a bitch to pay for what he had done to them. He wanted him to feel weak and as helpless as he did. There would be no greater joy then to see him squirming on the ground begging for his life or forgiveness just as he and his lover had. It was the worst thing he could think of that had ever happened to him. Most people would laugh at some shit like that but in Bentley's eyes, that shit was just like a grown man raping a little, down right unspeakable and wrong. His lover was long gone wanting to get over the situation on his own but Bentley couldn't let it go. He wasn't nervous or fearful of any consequences he just wanted him to suffer like he had to.

" Naw, Meech. This nigga had two nasty ass hoes rape me and my friend while they stood there laughing and shit like it was Def Comedy Jam. Now this motherfucka's gotta pay."

" Com' on B. Don't do this. Not like this."

"If I let him go, he'll just arrest me and I ain't going to jail Meech."

"Dude I'll get you the best lawyer money can buy. Just put the gun down man. Straight up."

Bentley thought about it, weighing his options. He knew Messiah wouldn't lie to him and would definitely get him the best lawyer but the question was would he be able to get him off? He didn't want to take any chances on the shit but at the same time he knew killing a cop wouldn't be the smartest thing he had ever done. Bentley blew his breath heavily in and out as if he was doing Lamaze then he slowly lowered the gun. Everyone let out a simultaneous sigh of relief.

"Smart boy. Prison time for killing a Federal Agent is usually death." Crosby said lowering his hands placing them on his hips.

"No, you can't go to jail B. Damn dude you be killin me sometimes. Now hand me the gun." Messiah said reaching out for it.

"Naw man this is my protection. Just in case some cracker ass cops come back trying to rape me again."

"Awe you fucking faggot, just hand his ass the gun before I stick my dick off in your mouth Blackie." Crosby laughed.

"Man!"

BOOM!

Want More From Nicety?
Check out these titles available on Kindle now!

COMING SOON!

CPSIA information can be obtained at www.ICGtesting.com
Printed in the USA
LVOW01s1539190215

427559LV00017B/846/P